"There's
have an affair."

He continued ruthlessly, "If it's been thirteen years since you've made love with anyone, you're long overdue. And I know I am."

Marnie stood very still, and of all the emotions churning in her belly, she couldn't have said which was uppermost. Desire? Fury? She said, finally, "That would be so easy for you, wouldn't it? Your daughter in Burnham and your mistress in Faulkner. Everything compartmentalized."

"Easy? No. But I can't deny that I want you. And I want you as my mistress far more than Kit needs you as a mother!"

Although born in England, **SANDRA FIELD** has lived most of her life in Canada: she says the silence and emptiness of the north speaks to her particularly. While she enjoys traveling, and passing on her sense of a new place, she often chooses to write about the city which is now her home. Sandra says, "I write out of my experience; I have learned that love with its joys and its pains is all-important. I hope this knowledge enriches my writing, and touches a chord in you, the reader."

Books by Sandra Field

HARLEQUIN PRESENTS®
2042—REMARRIED IN HASTE

Sandra Field

THE MOTHER OF HIS CHILD

HARLEQUIN®

TORONTO • NEW YORK • LONDON
AMSTERDAM • PARIS • SYDNEY • HAMBURG
STOCKHOLM • ATHENS • TOKYO • MILAN • MADRID
PRAGUE • WARSAW • BUDAPEST • AUCKLAND

ISBN 0-373-12144-X

THE MOTHER OF HIS CHILD

First North American Publication 2000.

Copyright © 1999 by Sandra Field.

This edition published by arrangement with Harlequin Books S.A.

® and TM are trademarks of the publisher. Trademarks indicated with
® are registered in the United States Patent and Trademark Office, the
Canadian Trade Marks Office and in other countries.

Visit us at www.eHarlequin.com

Printed in U.S.A.

CHAPTER ONE

MARNIE Carstairs pulled her car over on the shoulder of the road; the motor gave its usual asthmatic wheeze, then settled down to a low grumble. From her vantage point on the crest of the hill, she could see the town of Burnham spread out below. Her destination. The place that might answer—at least partially—some of the terrible questions she'd lived with for nearly thirteen years.

No wonder her hands were ice-cold and her throat tight with anxiety.

Burnham was a pretty town on this sunny Sunday in late April, situated as it was around the shores of an inlet of the Atlantic. Its houses and shops were painted bright colors, while its church spires pointed cheerfully to the high-piled clouds and the wheeling gulls. A few yachts admired their own reflections in the silky water, their hulls crisply painted white and blue. On the wooded hills that overlooked the town, Marnie could pick out the stone buildings of Burnham University. Did Calvin Huntingdon work there? Perhaps his wife did, too.

It was their names that had brought Marnie here today. Calvin and Jennifer Huntingdon of Burnham, Nova Scotia. Two names, a place and a date: the date of birth of Marnie's child all those years ago, the child who had been, against her knowledge and her every wish, adopted. The child she had not seen or heard of since then.

If her mother hadn't died at fifty-two, a death that no one had anticipated, least of all Charlotte Carstairs herself, Marnie would never have found that single piece of paper

5

in a plain white envelope in her mother's safe. She was sure of it. Her mother would have destroyed it.

The Huntingdons' names had been printed on the paper in Charlotte Carstairs's angular script, along with the birth date and the name of this little town: a discovery that had rocked Marnie to her roots.

The Huntingdons must have adopted her child. What other conclusion could she come to?

Briefly, the town blurred in her vision. She stared down at the steering wheel, noticing that her fingernails had dug tiny crescents into the vinyl covering, and that her wrists were taut from the strain of her grip. She had very strong fingers and wrists; for the past five years she'd been learning how to rock climb. Making a deliberate effort to relax, she blew out her breath in a long sigh, checked in the rearview mirror and engaged the clutch. No point in sitting here. She'd come this far, she'd at least follow through on the rest of her plan.

If you could call it a plan.

As she pulled back on the highway, she noticed that the bank of clouds to the southeast had lowered over the hills, the edges of the clouds swabbed with a theatrical blend of purple and gray. Storm clouds. Then a gust riffled the water and the yachts swayed uneasily at their moorings.

It wasn't an omen. Of course it wasn't.

The Huntingdons' address was engraved on Marnie's mind; she'd found it, all too easily, in the phone book. Her plan, such as it was, was to drive past the house and check it out; at least that way she'd see where her child was living.

And was she praying that a twelve-year-old girl would run out of the house just as she drove by?

Basically, she didn't have a plan. She'd come here because she couldn't possibly have done otherwise. No force on earth could have kept her away. Even though she was afraid that her action would tear open old wounds better left alone.

The Huntingdons would be wealthy; Charlotte Carstairs would have seen to that. No, Marnie had never worried about the material circumstances of the baby she had never seen. It was other concerns that had haunted her over the years. Was her daughter loved? Was she happy? Did she know she was adopted? Or did she believe that the two people bringing her up were her true parents?

Calvin Huntingdon her real father, and Jennifer her only mother.

Stop it, Marnie, she scolded herself. One step at a time. Check out the house first and then go from there. This is a small town; you can buy yourself a pizza at the local hangout and ask a few discreet questions about the Huntingdons. Stop for gas down the street and do the same thing there. No one can hide in a place the size of Burnham. You grew up in Conway Mills; you know all about small towns.

As if on a signal, the sun disappeared behind the clouds, Burnham's narrow main street darkening as if a blanket had been thrown over it. Or a shroud, she thought with a shiver of her nerves. If this were a movie, they'd be playing spooky music right now, the kind that warns you something really scary's going to happen.

She made it a policy to stay away from horror movies. The footsteps-coming-up-the-stairs-and-you-know-it's-the-bad-guy-with-an-ax kind of movie.

On impulse, Marnie turned into a paved parking lot to her left, which surrounded a small strip mall and an ice-cream stand decorated with little flags that were now snapping in the wind. Spring had come early to Nova Scotia this year. The day was unseasonably warm, and Marnie adored ice cream; it was number two on her list of comfort foods, right up there with barbecued chips. A flea market was going on in the mall, so the parking lot was fairly crowded. She drew up several rows away from the ice-cream stand, grabbed her purse and hurried between the parked vehicles. In front of the stand, half a dozen girls in jeans and anoraks were arguing about their favorite flavors; Marnie's heart gave a painful lurch, her eyes racing from one to the other of them. But they were all younger than twelve.

She didn't even know what her own child looked like.

Marnie bit hard on her lip and forced herself to scan the list of flavors. Another gust rattled the striped awning, and the last of the six girls took her cone from the attendant and put down her money.

"I'll have a double, please," Marnie said. "Cherry swirl on the bottom and mocha fudge on top."

It wasn't the time to worry about calories. She needed all the help she could get now that she was actually here in Burnham and she'd go for a jog on the beach when she got home tonight.

With a snap like a pellet, the first raindrop hit the awning. "Gonna have a little storm," the woman said affably. "But that's April for you. 'Bout as dependable as a kid on roller-blades."

The rain now sounded like a machine-gun attack. "Maybe it won't last long," Marnie offered.

"On again, off again, been like that the past few days. There you are, miss, that's two dollars."

Marnie paid, grabbed a wad of paper napkins and took a hefty bite from the mocha fudge. To give herself courage, she was wearing her new denim overalls with a turquoise turtleneck and matching turquoise flats. The sweater emphasized the unusual color of her eyes, which were also turquoise, rather like an ocean shoal on a summer's day.

Her earrings, big gold hoops, were almost hidden by a tumble of bright chestnut curls. The wind caught in her hair, tossing it around her head, and hurriedly she stepped back under the awning.

Although the rain showed no signs of abating, now that she was this close, Marnie craved action even if it was only to see the house. She said to the attendant, "Can you direct me to Moseley Street?"

"Sure thing. Go right through town to where the road forks. The left turn's Moseley. Wow—hear that thunder?"

"Thanks," Marnie said, lifting her face to the sky. All nature's excesses tended to exhilarate rather than frighten her. In a surge of optimism, she thought, I'll see where my daughter lives, I'll find out she has the best of parents, and I'll go home with my mind at rest. Knowing she's loved and happy.

Peace. Closure of a kind. She was long overdue for both.

She took another big hunk out of the ice cream and plunged out into the rain, her shoes slapping on the wet pavement. Raindrops stung her face, almost as if they were hail, her sweater sticking wetly to her skin. Head down, she raced for her car. Luckily, she hadn't bothered to lock it.

A dark green Cherokee was parked next to it. As she lunged for the door handle of her own car, a man suddenly appeared from behind the Cherokee, traveling fast, his head bent against the rain. Marnie yelped a warning, stopping in her tracks. The man looked up, but his momentum carried him forward so that he drove her hard against the driver's door. He was a big man. Her ice cream inscribed a neat arc in the air and plopped onto the hood of the Cherokee, leaving her holding the empty cone. Runnels of pink and brown splattered the shiny green paint, along with walnuts and little chunks of bright red maraschino cherries.

Marnie began to laugh, gurgles of infectious laughter that

made twin dimples appear in her cheeks. "Oh, no," she gasped, "cherries on the Cherokee. I *am* sorry, I wasn't watching where I was going and..." She broke off, puzzled. "What's wrong?"

The man still had her jammed against the door of her car. Water was dripping onto his forehead from his black hair, which was cut short and had a tendency to curl. His eyes were blue, so dark a blue as to be almost gray, and deep set. Like a quarry, Marnie thought, a slate quarry. His nose was crooked and his cheekbones wide-spaced: details that gave his face character. For he was—and she had decided this in the merest instant—the most attractive man she'd ever seen.

Attractive? He gave a whole new dimension to that word. Drop-dead gorgeous would be more like it.

He also seemed to have been struck dumb. His silence gave her time to feel through her clothing his lean muscularity and to appreciate his height—several inches taller than her five foot nine. He looked, she realized belatedly, as though he'd had a severe shock; nor had he, even momentarily, laughed at the ludicrous sight of her airborne ice cream. Suddenly frightened, she shoved against him and repeated, "What's the matter?"

Slowly, he straightened to his full height, his gaze glued to her face. She could feel her cheeks flush from more than her headlong run through the rain. In a hoarse voice, he demanded, "Who *are* you?"

It wasn't the response she'd expected. Distant lightning flickered across his face, shadowing the lines of strain around his mouth. He was pale under his tan and his eyes were blank: as though he'd been shaken to his foundations. Into the silence between lightning and thunder, Marnie countered, "What do you mean, who am I?"

He ran his fingers through his wet hair, disarranging it

still more. "Exactly what I say. I want to know your name and I want to know what you're doing here."

"Look," she said forcefully, "I'm sorry we bumped into each other and I'm sorry I got ice cream on your nice new car. But I've got enough napkins here to clean up four cars, and you bumped into me just as much as I bumped into—"

"Just answer the question."

Thunder rumbled melodramatically overhead. Marnie's eyes darted around her. No one else in sight. All the sensible people were indoors waiting for the rain to end. Which was precisely where she ought to be. "I don't have to answer any of your questions," she retorted. "Now if you'll excuse me—"

"I've got to know who you are!"

Exasperated, Marnie announced, "I'm not in the habit of telling strange men my name—especially ones as big and dangerous-looking as you."

"Dangerous?" he repeated blankly.

"You're darn right."

He took a deep, shuddering breath. "Listen, can we start over? And in the meantime, why don't we get in my car? You're getting soaked."

"Not on your life."

"You're reading me all wrong," he said, making an obvious effort to speak more normally. "I'm not trying to abduct you or harm you in any way—that's the last thing on my mind. But I've got to talk to you and we're both getting wetter by the moment. Here, I'll give you my car keys, then you'll know we're not going anywhere."

He fished in the pocket of his faded cords and produced a key ring, then passed it to her. Marnie took it automatically, although she was careful not to touch him. The keys were warm from his body. "I'd rather get wet, thank you very much,'' she said. ''No way am I getting in the vehicle of a total stranger. What do you think I am, nuts?''

For the first time, something like a smile loosened the taut lines of his face. ''If I didn't feel as though I've just had the rug pulled right out from under me, I might even see this as funny,'' he said. ''I'm an entirely respectable citizen of Burnham who's never once in the past fifteen years been seen as remotely dangerous. Not even around university administrators, who are enough to make a saint contemplate homicide. Although, when I think about it, there might be a few gun-toting guerrillas in Third-World countries who'd agree with you.''

Guerrillas? With guns? And he was trying to reassure her? She said tartly, ''Respectable citizen? Huh.'' In one quick glance, she took in the impressive width of his shoulders and the depth of his rib cage. ''You'd look right at home having a showdown with a bunch of thugs.''

''I assure you, I lead a blameless life,'' he said, a gleam of self-mockery in his slate blue eyes.

The lightning was a hard flash this time, much closer; Marnie's overalls were, by now, clinging clammily to her legs. She added, ''Anyway, you could have another set of keys in your other pocket.''

His smile grew wider and definitely more convincing. Yikes, Marnie thought, you shouldn't be allowed out, mister. The woman isn't born who could resist that smile. And she watched as he turned out both pockets and patted the pockets on his shirt to show they were empty. It was a blue shirt, now molded by the rain to his flat belly. ''Please,'' he said.

A raindrop trickled down the shallow cleft in his chin; he could have done with a shave, which added to his general air of unreliability.

Wondering if she was being a complete idiot, Marnie

unlocked the passenger door of the Cherokee and pushed the button to unlock all the other doors. A peal of thunder battered its way noisily across the parking lot. As she gave him one last suspicious scrutiny, he yelled, "Aren't you afraid of lightning storms?"

"No. It's large, angry men I'm afraid of," she yelled back. Then she climbed in the Cherokee, putting the keys in her pocket and waiting for him to get in. On the drive to Burnham, when she'd tried to imagine what might happen today, her wildest fantasies couldn't have come up with this scenario.

As he opened his door, he said, "I thought all women were scared of thunder."

"That's a huge generalization. I love thunderstorms, hurricanes and blizzards. Shut the door, you're letting the rain in."

He climbed in, slammed the door and turned toward her in his seat, raking her features almost as though he'd never seen a woman before; the smile had vanished. In a voice charged with suppressed emotion, he said, "What's your name, where are you from and what are you here for?"

"Why do you want to know all that?"

He hesitated perceptibly. "You...remind me of someone."

As her brain, finally, swung into action, Marnie's heart began to beat with sick, heavy strokes. There was only one reason why she should resemble someone he knew...wasn't there? Clenching her fists against her wet dungarees, feeling more afraid than she'd ever been in her life, she took a giant step into the unknown. "Do I remind you of a twelve-year-old girl who lives in this town?" she croaked.

CHAPTER TWO

THE man's mouth thinned. "I'm the one who's supposed to be asking the questions. For God's sake, tell me who you are!"

"My name's Marnie Carstairs. I live in Faulkner Beach—fifty miles down the coast." Although his eyes were as hard as stones, giving as little away, Marnie forced herself to take a second momentous step. "Is your name Calvin Huntingdon?"

In a ferocious whisper, he demanded, "How do you know who I am?"

She sagged back against the seat. He *was* Calvin Huntingdon. This was the man who'd lived with her child for nearly thirteen years. This was the man her daughter would call father. Her daughter existed. Lived right here in Burnham.

Tears flooded Marnie's eyes. She fought them back, she who had fought back so much emotion in her thirty years. Swallowing hard, staring at the rain that was streaming down the windshield, she asked her third question in the same tight voice. "Did you adopt a baby girl nearly thirteen years ago? She was born on the twenty-second of June."

His breath hissed through his teeth. As Marnie's eyes flickered over his features, she saw that once again he looked thoroughly dangerous. "How did you get my name?" he grated. "Adoption papers can only be accessed by the child, and only then as an adult."

"Does it matter?" she asked tonelessly. "It was by chance, that's all. Pure chance."

"You expect me to believe that? Come off it—what's the name of the game?"

Through the pain and confusion that was surging through her, Marnie felt the stirrings of anger. She scrubbed at her wet cheeks with the napkins that she still seemed to be clutching, sat up straighter and looked right at him. "There's something very wrong with this scene. I'm not on trial here!"

With a deadly quietness, he said, "Then why are you here?"

And how could she answer that? When she herself didn't know the answer. Hadn't gotten any further in her planning than to drive past the Huntingdons' house and to ask a few innocent questions of people who'd never link her with a child adopted all those years ago. And finally her mind made the connection that had been glaringly obvious ever since she'd collided with Calvin Huntingdon. "She...she looks like me," she stumbled. "My daughter...she looks like me."

Some of the tension eased from her body. A smile spread slowly over her face, a smile of such wonderment and joy that the depths of her irises were as translucent as the sea, and her soft, vulnerable mouth as gently curved as a new moon. Her daughter bore the marks of her true mother; was, in a very real way, her own flesh.

He said harshly, "Very touching. Are you an actress, Marnie Carstairs? Or do you just watch too many soap operas?"

Her jaw dropped. In a burst of antagonism, she snapped, "Do you treat her like this? My daughter? Doubting everything she says? Jeering at all her emotions? Because if so, then you're not fit to be her father."

"She's not your daughter! You gave up that right a long time ago."

"She'll always be my daughter," Marnie cried. "No one on earth can convince me otherwise—and certainly not you."

"So what about the father?" he lashed. "Where's he? Or are you saving him up for another day?"

"He's none of your business."

"Get real. Why have you turned up in Burnham thirteen years after the fact? What are you after—money? Is that it?"

To her own surprise, Marnie started to laugh. A ragged laugh, but a laugh nevertheless. "Right on—I'm after your money. Give me a million bucks or else I'll turn up on your doorstep and raise hell." Her voice rose. "How *dare* you? You don't know the first thing about me and you dare accuse me—"

"I know you gave up your child nearly thirteen years ago. It seems to me I know rather a lot about you, Miss Carstairs."

Marnie had gone too far for discretion. "She duped me, my mother. I thought I was going to marry my cousin Randall and all three of us would live together—me, Randall and the baby. Oh, God, it's such a long story and I was such a stupid little fool to trust her, but—"

"I'm sure it's a long story," he interrupted smoothly. "After all, you've had a long time to come up with it, haven't you? But oddly enough, it's not a story I want to hear. Just answer me one question. Why did you come here today?"

"You know what?" Marnie retorted with deliberate provocation, flags of temper reddening her cheeks, her breasts heaving under her wet sweater. "I don't like you, Calvin Huntingdon."

"You don't have to like me. And I don't go by Calvin. The name's Cal."

"Oh, sure," she said rudely. "So we're on a first-name basis. Isn't that just ducky?"

"I'll tell you one thing," he said. "I'm beginning to realize where my daughter comes by her temper. And her red hair."

"My hair isn't red," Marnie snapped childishly. "It's auburn. Which is quite different." The storm of emotion in her breast craving release, she gave him a narrow-eyed scrutiny. "And you just blew it—because you didn't have the slightest intention of telling me one single thing about her, did you, Mr. Huntingdon?"

"No, I wasn't going to tell you anything," he said savagely. "But there's something about you—you sure know how to get under my skin. So why don't I go for broke and tell you something else I've discovered in the past few minutes? She'll be beautiful, my daughter. Quite extraordinarily beautiful."

Marnie wasn't often struck speechless; she worked, after all, as a librarian in a junior high school where repartee was part of her strategy for keeping the lid on her students. But right now she couldn't think of one word to say. To her intense dismay, she felt a blush creep up her cheeks all the way to her hairline. To her equally intense dismay, his compliment—for compliment it was—gave her a thrill of pleasure deep down in that place she never allowed a man to go.

Cal banged his fist on the steering wheel. "I don't believe I just said that."

Finding her voice, Marnie said shrewishly, "Your wife would be most impressed," and tried to keep her mind off both his wife and his profile, which was every bit as attractive as the rest of him. His nose had a little bump in it, and his chin—well, arrogant would be one word to describe that hard line of bone. Arrogant. Masculine in the extreme. Sexy.

Sexy? A man's jaw? What was the matter with her?

A married man, moreover. Who—the ultimate irony—happened to be the father of her child.

The jaw she had just been admiring tightened ominously. "Let's leave my wife out of this and get back to the essentials. Why you're here. What you want from me."

"Oh," she said gently, "what I want is something I'm not going to get. That's very clear."

"Okay, I'll bite. What is it?"

"Compassion, Cal. Simple compassion. That's all."

She had, she saw, taken him by surprise. She didn't know Cal Huntingdon very well, but she was sure it wasn't often that he was knocked off balance. Especially by a woman. He said flatly, "Compassion has to be earned."

"Then I'll tell you why I'm here. I wanted to see the house where my daughter lives. I'd hoped to ask a few questions of the locals, find out what you're like. You and your wife. To see—" her voice shook in spite of herself "—if my child is happy."

"And that's all?"

She hated him for so openly doubting her. "Do you honestly believe I'd turn up on your doorstep without a word of warning?" she flared. "Oh, hello, I happen to be your daughter's biological mother and I was just passing by and thought I'd drop in. For heaven's sake, I don't even know if she realizes she's adopted! What kind of woman do you think I am?"

"I'd have to have the brains of Einstein to answer that."

"Does she know? That she's adopted?" Marnie whispered, twisting her hands painfully in her lap as she waited for him to sneer at her again, to deny her information that was crushingly important to her.

"Look at me, Marnie." There was a note in his voice new to her. She raised her head and saw, momentarily, something that was perhaps compassion. He said quietly, "Yes, she knows she's adopted. We were truthful with her about that from the start. We thought it best in the long run."

Marnie blinked back another flood of tears. "Do you see what that means?" she blundered. "It means that—even if minimally—she knows I exist."

"You and the man who fathered her."

Two tears dripped on her clasped fingers. Refusing to acknowledge them, Marnie said steadily, "That's right."

He said evenly, "There's one thing you haven't asked me."

"*Is* she happy?"

"I didn't mean that. You haven't asked me her name. The name we gave our daughter."

More tears welled up on her lashes. She'd been afraid to ask. "So what did you call her, Cal?"

"Katrina. Katrina Elizabeth. She goes by Kit."

Suddenly, it was all too much for Marnie. Desperate to be alone, she fumbled for the door handle. Blinded by tears, sobs strangling her breathing, she yanked on the catch. Cal caught her by the shoulder. Frantically, she twisted free of him. "Let go! I can't take any more of this."

And then the door was open and she was tumbling to the ground, her feet splashing in a puddle, the wind snarling her hair. She slammed the door shut and lunged for her own car, scrambling into her seat and instinctively jamming down the lock button on her side and the passenger side. It was a two-door car. She was safe. Only then did Marnie bow her head onto the steering wheel and begin to weep, sobbing as though there was no tomorrow.

* * *

Dimly, Marnie realized someone was banging on the window. Had been for some time. She looked up, blinking through her wet lashes. The rain had lessened, pattering softly on the windshield. Cal was rapping on the glass with his fist. He was very wet. He must have been standing there the whole time, watching her sob her heart out.

Invading her privacy.

She rolled her window partway down and said jaggedly, "I am not going to turn up on your doorstep, and once I've filled the car up with gas I'm going home. Goodbye, Mr. Huntingdon."

"Oh, no," he said softly, "it's not quite that simple. Before you go anywhere, I want you to swear you won't try to get in touch with Kit."

"I wouldn't be that irresponsible!"

"Swear, Marnie."

If looks could kill, his would have blitzed her in her seat. Pushing her hair back from her face, Marnie scowled right back. She needed to blow her nose. Which, she knew from past experience, was undoubtedly bright pink after her crying jag. "I won't do anything to harm my daughter. And you'll have to be satisfied with that—because it's all you're getting from me."

She turned the key in the ignition, and for once her car started on the first try. But as she reached for her seat belt, Cal inserted his hand through the gap, yanked on the lock button and pulled her door open. He barked, "You're not calling the shots here—I am. As Kit's father. You say you're going to get gas. You think they won't look at you down at the station and see Kit Huntingdon written all over you? You're a walking time bomb, and I want you to promise you'll head out of Burnham right now and you won't come back. Do you hear?"

His voice had risen during this speech; Marnie might not

care for large, angry men, but on the other hand she wasn't about to show Cal Huntingdon she was shivering all the way to her very wet shoes. "All right, I'll buy my gas out of town! Now will you please shut the door and let me get out of here before anyone sees me? The last thing you should be doing is holding me up. What if a friend of yours comes along?"

A muscle twitched in his jaw. "The next time I come to the supermarket for milk on a Sunday, I'll think twice," he snarled. "Remember what I said, Marnie Carstairs. Get out of Burnham and stay out. And don't you dare try to get in touch with Kit."

He slammed the door in her face. She pushed the clutch into first gear, flicked on the wipers and drove away without a backward glance, her fingers gripping the steering wheel as though it were Cal's throat. At the exit to the parking lot, she turned right. Right led her out of town. Away from the local gas station and away from Moseley Street.

Away from Katrina Elizabeth Huntingdon, her daughter. Known as Kit. And away from Cal and Jennifer Huntingdon, the couple who nearly thirteen years ago had adopted her.

It would take a woman of extraordinarily strong character to live with Cal. What was Jennifer Huntingdon like? And was she a good mother?

Was she beautiful? It was unlikely Cal would be married to someone who wasn't. Yet he'd called her, Marnie, beautiful.... Why had he done that?

A mile out of town, when she'd passed the vinyl-sided Baptist Church and the boutiques temptingly arrayed for the tourists, Marnie pulled into a take-out stand. It was one-thirty. She hadn't had lunch, and her ice cream had ended up on Cal's Cherokee instead of in her stomach. She'd buy a sandwich. And then she'd do some hard thinking.

She took her sandwich to a small picnic spot along the shore, choosing the end table so she'd have privacy. The rain had stopped; the undergrowth smelled damp and pungent. She sat down on the wet bench and started to eat. Cal shouldn't have tried ordering her about. She'd never liked being told what to do. Charlotte Carstairs had been long on orders and short on love, and there was no question in Marnie's mind but that her own child had been conceived—at least partly—out of rebellion.

The sandwich tasted good. Chickadees were chattering companionably among the trees, and waves lapped on the rocks. Gradually, Marnie calmed down, all her new knowledge settling more gently into her mind. Her daughter's name was Kit. Kit looked so like Marnie that Cal had ordered Marnie out of town. Because he didn't want anyone knowing about Kit's real mother. He certainly didn't want to run any risk of Kit and Marnie meeting.

Which hurt. Hurt quite dreadfully.

With a jolt, Marnie suddenly remembered the one question Cal hadn't answered. An extremely important question. In fact, the most essential question of them all. Whether Kit was happy.

He'd sidestepped it by telling Marnie Kit's name. Whereupon she'd cried a bucket and forgotten to ask the question again. Was it just a genuine oversight on his part? Or had he had other motives? Motives of deception? Darker motives.

Chewing on her chicken salad, Marnie let a picture of Cal Huntingdon fill her mind. Unconsciously, and even in the midst of that turmoil of emotion in the parking lot, she realized that ever since they'd met she'd been searching for the one word that would encapsulate him. She'd come up with arrogant, sexy and masculine, and certainly each of those was accurate enough. Dangerous seemed entirely apt, as well. But something else was nagging at her mind, making her deeply uneasy. For some reason, she found herself remembering how facetiously she'd thought about the sort of scary movie she hated: the man-with-an-ax-coming-up-the-stairs kind. The bad guy.

She didn't for one minute think Cal was a potential ax murderer. No, that wasn't what she was getting at. But he did pose an enormous threat to her at a level that was gut-deep.

Was it his willpower? He had that all right. He'd hated her defying him.

Take away the first syllable of willpower, she thought, and what have you got? Power. That was it. The man reeked of power. His body, his voice, his actions—all of them were imbued with the unconscious energy of a man used to wielding power.

Charlotte Carstairs had been in love with power all her life. It had taken a huge and ongoing effort on Marnie's part to prevent that power from ruining her own life, from making her as bitter and unloving as her mother.

Marnie finished her sandwich, drained the bottle of apple juice she'd bought to go with it and got back into her car. She rummaged in her haversack, found the square scarf that went with her raincoat and wrapped it, turban-style, around her head, carefully tucking her hair under it. She fished out her dark glasses and generously coated her lips with Strawberry Pearl Glaze. With some satisfaction, she looked at herself in the mirror. She did not look like the woman who'd bought an ice cream cone in the pouring rain.

Then she turned out of the picnic spot and headed back toward Burnham.

This time, she did have a plan.

She drove slowly through the town, her eyes peeled for a dark green Cherokee. At the gas station, she pulled up to the pumps and asked for a fill-up, adding casually, "I'm looking for Cal Huntingdon. Can you tell me where he lives?"

"Sure thing. Go to the fork in the road and hang a left. Moseley Street. His place is about a kilometer from the fork. Big cedar-shingled bungalow on the cove. Nice place. Want your oil checked, miss?"

"No, it's fine, thanks." As the red numbers clicked on the pump, she said with complete untruth, "I used to know him in my college days. Haven't seen him for a while."

"Yeah? Too bad about his wife, eh?"

Marnie's fingers tightened around her credit card. "I—I hadn't heard…is something wrong? I was in the area today and thought I'd drop in on them."

"Well, now…she passed away two years ago. Cancer. Took her real fast, which is a blessing, I guess."

"Oh," said Marnie. "Oh. I'm sorry. I didn't know."

"Hard on the kid. And on Cal, too, of course. That's twenty-five even, miss."

Feeling thoroughly ashamed of herself, Marnie handed over her card and a few moments later signed the slip. "I may phone first," she said. "Rather than just dropping in. Thanks for telling me."

"No problem. You have a nice day now."

"Nice" wasn't quite the word Marnie would have used to describe the day she was having. Her heart was racketing around in her chest again. She turned out of the gas station and asked the first person she saw for directions to the junior high school. Within ten minutes, she had a mental picture of the layout of the town and had figured out the probable route Kit Huntingdon would take to walk from Moseley Street to the consolidated school. Only then did Marnie leave Burnham.

She hadn't seen a green Cherokee. And she'd be the first

to admit she lacked the courage to drive past the cedar-shingled house on the cove.

Cal Huntingdon was a widower. Had been for two years. Which meant, unless he had a live-in girlfriend, that Kit was motherless.

Even though intuition told her Cal wasn't the type for a live-in girlfriend, not when he had an adolescent daughter, that same intuition insisted that any woman worth her salt would be after him. Wanting to comfort him. In bed and out.

Bed? Don't go there, Marnie. Not when Cal's on your mind. Cal plus bed could be a combination several steps beyond dangerous. You swore off men years ago, and even thinking about Cal Huntingdon in a sexual context is lunacy. Kit's the issue here, and only Kit.

He hadn't told her the truth. He'd allowed her to think that Kit had two parents, a mother as well as a father. That everything was normal and as it should be in the Huntingdon household. Mother, father, daughter—and no place for Marnie.

Beneath a very real sorrow for an unknown woman who had died far too young, Marnie was aware of anger, red-hot and seething. Kit had been left, tragically, without a mother. And yet Cal had dared to warn off the woman who had borne Kit all those years ago, a woman who had, surely, some claim on his honesty.

Some claim on Kit.

CHAPTER THREE

ON MONDAY morning, just before eight, Marnie arrived at the fork in the road that led out of Burnham. Moseley Street, the sign said. She flicked on her signal light and turned left. She was driving her best friend Christine's small white Pontiac; she'd phoned Christine last night and asked if they could trade cars for the day.

Cal Huntingdon wouldn't even notice if a white Pontiac drove past his house.

She checked the odometer, her heart hammering in her chest as loudly as a woodpecker on a tree. The Huntingdons lived about a kilometer down the road, according to the man at the gas station. It was a pretty road, following the curve of the bay and lush with evergreens. Point-seven kilometers, point-eight, point-nine. And then Marnie saw the cedar-shingled house on the cove, the mailbox neatly lettered "Huntingdon."

She braked. Although a dark green Cherokee was parked in front of the house, there was no one in sight, neither Cal nor a young girl hurrying up the driveway on her way to school.

It was the house of her dreams.

Marnie's mouth twisted. She'd had a lot of dreams over the years, several of which she'd made real—by guts, determination and plain hard work. But she was a long way from realizing this particular one. For the house spelled money.

It was a low bungalow, following the sloping contours of the land and taking full advantage of a spectacular view of a rocky cove. Pines and hemlocks shaded the roof; through the bare limbs of maples, sunlight glittered on the waves. The weathered cedar shingles blended perfectly with the surroundings. The chimney was built of chunks of native stone, while the slate pathways were the color of Cal's eyes.

It was perfect, Marnie thought. Utterly perfect.

In terms of material goods, Kit was obviously in another league from Marnie. Discovering she didn't like this thought one bit, Marnie put her foot to the accelerator and continued down the road, reluctantly noticing that the Huntingdon property extended several hundred feet farther along the cove. But why was she surprised that Kit had been adopted into money? She'd known all along that her mother worshiped money and even more the power it conferred; Charlotte wouldn't have placed her grandchild with anyone who lived in poverty.

In her will, Charlotte had left Marnie the sum of one hundred dollars. The rest of her estate had been allocated to build a town hall and a library in Conway Mills. The will had been dated the day of Kit's birth; a matter of hours after the birth, when Marnie's world was disintegrating around her, Charlotte had informed Marnie that she was disinherited.

At the time, money had been the furthest thing from Marnie's thoughts. But at the reading of the will, only a month ago, Charlotte's unchanging bitterness toward her only daughter had had the power to wound deeply. Forgiveness, thought Marnie, was the most difficult of concepts. Had she herself ever really forgiven her mother?

Irritably, she wriggled the tightness from her shoulders and turned around in the third driveway beyond the Huntingdon place. As she drove past the bungalow again, there still was no sign of any occupants. Time for phase two, she decided grimly, and headed back into town. Ten minutes later, she was tucked into a window booth in the coffee-and-doughnut shop on the corner of the street by the junior high school. If she was right, Kit would walk along this street.

The sun, fortunately, was shining from a cloudless sky and again it was overly warm for late April. Marnie was wearing her largest pair of sunglasses and a big floppy hat under which she'd tucked most of her hair; it also hid her face. She'd taken the precaution of buying the daily paper in case she had to hide behind it.

She felt excruciatingly nervous. It was one thing to drive past the house where Kit lived; quite another to actually see her daughter.

Although she hated horror movies, Marnie loved James Bond. This morning, she was discovering she'd make a lousy espionage agent. She felt as though everyone in the place was staring at her and as though Kit, were she to go past the window, would pick her out unerringly.

She couldn't allow that to happen. Wouldn't allow it. All she wanted was to see her daughter. For the very first time. See if she was happy.

Was that too much to ask?

Last night, she'd phoned the principal of her school to tell him some urgent family business had come up and she needed the next day off. So here she was on a Monday morning in a coffee shop in Burnham when she should have been in the school library sorting books and checking out the computers.

Kids were now straggling past the coffee shop in loose groups, some with headsets, all in the regulation designer-label jeans and jackets with bright logos. Marnie sipped on coffee that could have been lye and unfolded the newspaper. Maybe Kit had a friend at the other end of town and walked to school a whole different way. Or else she might go by so fast Marnie wouldn't have time to recognize her.

She certainly couldn't chase after her.

A group of girls came around the corner of the building, their heads together, their laughter loud enough to be heard through the glass. One of them was tall with red hair, curly red hair that bounced in the sunlight.

Turn around, Marnie prayed. So I can see your face. Oh, please, turn around.

As though the girl had heard her, she pointed at the array of doughnuts in the showcase and said something Marnie couldn't catch but that made all the other girls laugh. The girl's face was almost a replica of Marnie's, right down to the tilted nose and high cheekbones, except that her eyes were a warm brown. The color of Terry's eyes.

It was Kit. Unquestionably it was Kit.

Then, to her horror, Marnie saw the whole group veer toward the door of the coffee shop. She grabbed her newspaper and lifted it, hiding her face, her fingers trembling. Although she braced her elbows on the table and willed her hands to steadiness, they wouldn't obey her.

The bottom of the door scraped on the black plastic floor mat. "What kind of doughnut, Kit?" one of the girls called out.

"Double chocolate. Maybe that way I'll stay awake in math class."

The others giggled. Another voice said, "Boston cream for me. Kit, did you study for the test?"

"Yeah...my dad made me."

One of the others groaned in sympathy. "My mum did, too. I wanted to watch a MuchMusic video instead." In a wicked parody of an adult's voice, she went on, "'Not until the weekend, Lizzie.' Mothers are such a drag."

"Shut up, Lizzie," Kit flared.

"Oops, sorry," Lizzie said. "I'll have a maple cream and share it with you, Kit."

"Okay. You know what? I'm going to ace that test," Kit said confidently. "I've got to keep my marks up or I'm off the basketball team. Dad said so."

Kit's voice was light, higher-pitched than Marnie's. Willing herself to stop shaking, Marnie listened as the girls paid for their doughnuts and trooped out of the coffee shop. Over the top of the paper she caught one last glimpse of Kit. She was taking a big bite out of the double chocolate doughnut; she was wearing Levi's and a baggy purple sweatshirt. Marnie's favorite color was purple.

Marnie sat still, gazing blindly at the newsprint, trying to assimilate the fact that after thirteen years she had actually seen her daughter. Heard her voice. Had evidence, she thought wryly, of Kit's quick temper, so like Marnie's. Kit hadn't liked Lizzie's remark about mothers. Did that mean Kit still missed her mother? It must.

What had Jennifer Huntingdon been like? Warm and loving? Strong-willed? Happy?

A gang of teenage boys rocketed through the door, their energy making Marnie wince. She listened as they argued about doughnuts, then watched them leave with relief. What did Kit think about boys? Was she interested in them yet? Or did basketball interest her more?

You'll never know the answer to those questions, Marnie. Because Kit is Cal's daughter, not yours.

Slowly, Marnie lowered the newspaper, trying desperately to ignore the storm of emotion engulfing her whole body. Now what? she wondered. What do I do next?

When she'd decided last night that she was going back to Burnham despite Cal's warnings, she hadn't gotten any further than seeing Kit. Well, she'd seen her. Seen her friends, noticed her clothes, heard her voice. That's it,

Marnie. Kit's happy enough, even if she does still miss her mother. Certainly she's well looked after financially. You've done everything you can do. Now you've got to return to Faulkner and stay away from Burnham. The last thing you can risk is bumping into your daughter on the street. You can't do that to her. It would be utterly unfair.

Moving like a woman much older than thirty, Marnie left her unfinished coffee and her newspaper on the table and walked out of the shop. She was going to drive home and cry her eyes out for the second time in as many days. She hardly ever cried. But that was what she was going to do.

It didn't make much sense to cry—after all, she now had a face and a voice for her daughter where yesterday she'd had nothing—but she knew she had to do it. She ached all over, as though someone had pounded her body mercilessly in her sleep: an ache both physical and emotional, the same ache she'd suffered in that hospital bed in the private clinic so many years ago.

As she turned up a side street, she passed from sunlight into shade. She didn't see the man standing statue-still between the two nearest buildings; rather, she was reaching into the pocket of her jeans for the keys to Christine's car, her mind anywhere but on her surroundings. Not until a tanned, strong-fingered and unmistakably masculine hand fastened itself around her elbow was she jerked out of her reverie. "You're coming with me," Cal Huntingdon said in a clipped voice infused with rage, "and don't bother arguing."

With a strange sense of inevitability, Marnie looked up. Had she really thought she'd get away with her caper in the coffee shop? Saying the first thing that came into her head, she muttered, "I didn't see the Cherokee."

"I parked it on the next street. I didn't see that wreck you're driving, either. Come on."

He was pulling on her arm as though she were eight years old. She said coldly, "I'm perfectly capable of walking to your car. Let go."

"No."

Although he hadn't loosened his grip, Cal did stop tugging so hard. His fingers were warm; as she marched along beside him, Marnie discovered to her dismay that she liked the contact. Liked his height, the way his gray shirt was rolled up to his elbows, the tanned column of his throat. Scared to death by this realization, she said defiantly, "You didn't see my car because I borrowed a friend's."

"I figured you'd pull a stunt like that. Which is why I was watching for you."

"Don't you think you should be at work? To pay for the very expensive house I drove past this morning?"

"It's paid for, Marnie Carstairs. Every shingle and tree root. I'm surprised you didn't bang on the door to check out the furniture."

To her annoyance, Marnie couldn't come up with a retort that would sound anything other than pettish. They'd reached the Cherokee; she climbed in and fastened her seat belt. As Cal turned on the ignition, she said with deliberate provocation, "Where are we going? Home for coffee?"

"Don't push your luck," he growled, then pulled out into the street.

"Or are you planning to fling me over the nearest cliff?"

"I've thought of it, believe me," he said tightly. "We're getting the hell out of Burnham and then we're going to have a talk. During which I shall make a few things clear to you. In the meantime, why don't you just shut up?"

It seemed like good advice. Marnie gazed out the window as though the drugstore across the street was the most interesting building she'd ever seen.

Once they'd left Burnham, Cal turned onto the highway that would lead eventually to Faulkner Beach. When he came to the picnic spot where Marnie had eaten her lunch the day before, he wheeled into it. There were no other cars there. Why would there be? thought Marnie. Most people don't picnic for breakfast. He even chose the same table as she had.

She slid out of the Cherokee and sat down on top of the table, facing the sea, her feet resting on the bench. The buds were still tight on the trees, although a song sparrow was piping its melody from a nearby birch. The ocean glinted as though it were alive, the waves chuckling among the rocks. "No cliffs," she said. "That's a relief."

Cal stationed himself in front of her, his back to the water. Shoulders hunched, hands jammed in the pockets of his jeans, he looked at her unwaveringly. His gray shirt was open at the throat as though he was immune to the cool ocean breeze; his hair shone with cleanliness, and he was clean shaven. He did not, Marnie noticed, look the slightest bit amused by her pert remark. Not that she really felt pert. She wasn't sure how she felt.

She'd probably find out in the next few minutes. Cal Huntingdon would see to that.

Without saying a word, Cal reached out and pulled her dark glasses off her nose, then folded them carefully and put them on the table beside her. Then he undid the cord on her hat, the back of his hand brushing her chin, and took the hat off, placing it on the table, too. Her hair tumbled around her ears. And the whole time, his eyes were intent on her features.

Her lashes flickered involuntarily. His face was so close

to hers she could see the small white scar over one eye and catch the faint mint scent of his aftershave.

She'd expected a tirade from him. Not this.

She had absolutely no idea what he was thinking.

Marnie stared back at him, forcing herself to keep her hands loose in her lap and struggling to hide her inner trembling. His action, so unexpected, had broken through a boundary that she guarded fiercely. Her voice faltering, she said, "What you just did—that's got nothing to do with Kit."

Cal didn't bother denying it. "The sun in your hair...it's like little strands of copper."

The timbre of his voice, dusky as red wine, brought a flush to her cheeks. His eyes now looked more blue than gray and not at all like slate. She found herself gazing at his mouth, a generous mouth, cleanly sculpted, and wondering what it would be like to be kissed by him. To kiss him back.

He said levelly, "Don't worry, I'm thinking exactly the same thing."

Kiss him? She must be out of her mind. Cal was the enemy, the man determined to keep her from her daughter. Marnie shrank back. "Stay away from me."

Thrusting his hands into his pockets again, Cal said in a raw voice, "What's the matter? Not part of your game plan, Marnie?"

He'd gone so fast from what she would've sworn was desire to what she knew was rage that she felt dizzy. Which emotion was real? Only the anger? Had the desire been merely a facade? She rested her palms flat on the table, needing the solidity of wood to give her some kind of balance, and said with as much dignity as she could muster, "You took me by surprise."

"You'll forgive me, I'm sure," he said with heavy irony,

"if I don't believe you. I think it would take a lot to surprise you. When I stationed myself on the street where Kit
walks to school, I was telling myself I was every kind of
a fool. You'd said you wouldn't do anything to harm her—
I assumed that meant you'd stay away from Burnham. Not
risk her meeting you and seeing the resemblance between
you. In other words, I trusted you." He rocked back and
forth on the balls of his feet. "But I was wrong, wasn't I?
You're not to be trusted. This morning, you put yourself in
a situation where you ended up twenty feet away from my
daughter. I'd call that taking a risk, wouldn't you?"

Her own temper rose to meet his. "So we're talking
about trust, are we, Cal? Why didn't you tell me you're a
widower?"

Visibly, he flinched. "How did you find that out?"

"I asked. At the gas station in Burnham last night." She
raised her chin. "I don't like being ordered around."

"Not even when it's for the good of your daughter?"

"You have to allow me some part in that decision."

"I didn't tell you I'm a widower for the very obvious
reason that I wanted you out of town. Out of my life. Mine
and Kit's."

Marnie pushed her palms hard against the wooden table;
his eyes were those of a man in torment, his jaw an unyielding line. How he must have loved his wife: a realization that filled her inexplicably with envy. She'd never
known that kind of love and doubted she ever would.
Forcing herself to continue, she asked, "Are you living
with someone else? Or is Kit motherless?"

"That's got nothing to do with you."

"It's got everything to do with me!"

"You're forgetting something. You gave up your rights
to Kit when she was born."

Although her palms were sweating, the rest of Marnie

felt ice-cold. Knowing she was fighting for her life, she said in a cracked voice, "I turned seventeen three months before Kit was born. Until this morning, I'd never even laid eyes on her."

"Unfortunately, some decisions we make in life are irrevocable. Haven't you figured that out yet?"

"Are you really that hard, Cal?" she whispered. "Is there no room in you for human frailty?"

He said flatly, "I'd guard Kit's peace of mind with my very life."

Marnie pounced. "So is she happy? Tell me she's totally happy with her life the way it is, and I'll go away. I promise."

Abruptly, he swung away from her, gazing out to sea. The breeze toyed with his hair; his shoulders were rigid with tension.

Swiftly, Marnie stood up, putting herself between him and the water. In unconscious pleading, she rested her hand on his bare arm and said, "I hate this, Cal...this feeling we've got to score off each other, that Kit is some kind of prize we're fighting over, when surely what we both want is what's best for her. Can't we do this some other way?"

"There's no other woman in my house," he said evenly. "Do you really think I'd live with someone else so soon after Jennifer died? It would be the worst thing in the world for Kit."

And for him, too? Was that what he meant?

"Look at me, Cal." As he reluctantly obeyed, Marnie said, "I'm sorry your wife died. I'm truly sorry."

Her turquoise eyes were wide with sincerity and her fingers still lay loosely on his arm. "You mean that, don't you?"

"Of course I do. She was so young. It must have been dreadful for you—and for Kit."

He said in a voice from which all emotion had been removed, "That's why I can't risk your meeting Kit. She changed after Jennifer died. She started questioning everything and bucking authority, and she'd spend hours in her room listening to music and refusing to talk to me. I didn't know how to handle her. Still don't. She's not ready for another emotional upheaval, Marnie. You've got to believe me. She's not."

With a huge effort, Marnie kept her voice even. "I do believe you." She believed something else: that very likely Cal was also talking about himself.

Quickly, Cal covered her fingers with his own. "What I just said—it hurt, didn't it? Because it means you can't see Kit again. God, this is such a mess...."

"Just the same, I'm glad you told me about her."

Absently, he was playing with her hand. It was her left hand. "No rings?" he said. "But you must be married."

"Oh, no," she said, and snatched her hand back. "I've never married. Never wanted to."

His eyes were suddenly appalled. "Surely to God you weren't raped? That's not how Kit—"

"No! No, of course not. Her father's a good man, always was. He didn't even know about Kit until I told him five years ago. I never told him at the time."

"Why didn't you? Why didn't you marry him when she was born? If he was such a good man."

Marnie reached up and plucked a branch from the birch tree that brushed her arm, systematically starting to tear the buds apart with her nails. "Yesterday you virtually accused me of making up stories about how I lost Kit," she said in a low voice. "Give me one good reason why should I tell you about it now."

He took the twig from her fingers and dropped it to the ground. "Let's go down to the beach, sit on the rocks," he said, and for the first time that morning smiled at her. "We both need a break."

His smile transformed him, investing him with a wholly masculine vitality to which Marnie couldn't help but respond. As she gaped at him, he added quizzically, "Did I say something wrong?"

It's me that's in the wrong, thought Marnie. Thirteen years ago, I swore off sex and now I'm practically fainting at Cal's feet. Why do I keep forgetting that he's Kit's father? "No, no," she sputtered. "No, you didn't. I—I just can't figure you out, that's all."

"I'm just an ordinary guy, Marnie."

She snorted. "And the sea's made of cherry swirl ice cream."

He began to laugh. "It took me a whole box of Kleenex to clean off my car. Do you always mix your flavors?"

If his smile was sexy, his laugh was dynamite. "Always," she said. "Life's too short to play it safe."

Her words hung in the air between them. "So you believe that, too, do you?" Cal said. "Is *that* how Kit was conceived?"

Her smile died. "It always comes back to that, doesn't it?"

"You know what keeps throwing me?" he said with underlying violence. "You look so like Kit and yet you don't. You're a woman, where Kit's hovering between child and adolescent. You've suffered—don't think I can't see that—and it's given you a beauty that's been tested. A beauty that's far more than a question of good bones, skin like silk, eyes as blue as the sea." His gaze raked her from head to foot. "Along with legs that go on forever and a body that could drive a man crazy..." Running his fingers through his hair, he finished explosively, "Dammit, I never meant to say any of this! But there's something about you that takes all the rules and turfs them out the window.''

Frightened out of her wits, Marnie blurted, ''If you have rules, so do I. We can't afford to forget them, either one of us, because of your daughter. Your daughter and mine.''

''You think I don't know that?'' he blazed.

''This isn't about you and me,'' she persisted wildly. ''It's about Kit.'' She was right, she knew she was. Not since that one time had she ever let a man seduce her, not with words or with his body. So what was so different about Cal Huntingdon?

Power, she thought with an inward shiver. The power of his words, which had both terrified and exhilarated her. And, she admitted unwillingly, the power of his body. His height, the way his muscles moved in his throat when he swallowed, the gleam of sunlight across his cheekbones... Oh God, what was wrong with her? She'd never in her life been so aware of a man's sheer physicality.

Why did it have to be Cal, of all people, who was causing her to break all her self-imposed rules?

Be careful, Marnie. Be very careful. It's Kit you want. Not Kit's father.

Unable to stand the direction her thoughts had taken her, Marnie pushed her way through the bayberry shrubs onto the rocks.

Cal was right. She did need a break.

meant to say any of that, but you're so touchy about you that takes all the rules and . . . huh, there I go . . . windows . . .

CHAPTER FOUR

THE beach was made of shale, gray blue shale on which the blue green waves were advancing and retreating. Like Cal's eye color and her own, Marnie thought edgily. Finding a smooth boulder, she perched herself on it.

Cal bent and picked up a sliver of rock, then threw it so it skipped over the water half a dozen times before it sank. He said absently, "Kit loves to do that. Hers usually bounce more than mine—she's really got the knack."

Then he turned to face Marnie, his face clouded. "I knew she had a math test today, so I made her stay in last night to study when she wanted to be out with her friends. And do you know what she said? Her mother wouldn't have made her stay in, her mother hadn't been mean to her like me, she went on and on, and the irony is that Jennifer was stricter with her than I am. A couple of months ago, we went to a counselor, but Kit refused to even open her mouth. My best friend's wife has done her best to draw Kit out—same result. I normally travel three or four times a year as an adjunct to my job, but I've even cut that out, figuring she needs me home." His laugh was tinged with bitterness. "She needs me like she needs a hole in the head. It's almost as though she hates me for being alive now that Jennifer's dead."

Her heart aching, Marnie ventured, "She seemed happy enough with her friends this morning. She did tell Lizzie you'd made her study, but she didn't sound too upset about it."

"I warned her she'd be off the school basketball team if

her math marks didn't improve. She's their star forward, so she won't risk that.''

Even though as an adult Marnie preferred solitary pursuits to team sports, she'd played basketball when she was a teenager, and now she helped out with the Faulkner Fiends, the junior high girls' basketball team in her own school. One more link to Kit, she thought unhappily.

"Lately, she's even…" Then Cal broke off, picking up another rock and firing it at the water. It hit at the wrong angle and sank with a small splash.

"Even what?" Marnie prompted.

Restlessly, he shrugged his shoulders. "Never mind. Tell me how the adoption came about.''

She winced. "What's the point if I can't see Kit again?"

"Maybe it'll help me understand.''

"You don't need to understand, Cal! Because I'm finally getting the message. I've got to go home and forget my daughter lives fifty miles down the road.''

"Why did you give her up, Marnie?''

The breeze was freshening, molding Marnie's shirt to her breasts and teasing her hair. She stood up, rubbing her palms down the sides of her jeans. "I didn't. My mother deceived me—I told you that.''

"So tell me more.''

She stared out at the horizon. Wisely or unwisely, she knew she was going to do as he asked. But because she'd never told anyone but Terry about her pregnancy, and because it was all so long ago and yet so painfully present, her voice sounded clipped and unconvincing, even to her own ears. "Terry and I were best friends all through school. Most of the kids either hated me or avoided me because of my mother. She owned the mill. Everyone in the town owed their livelihood to the mill. Try that one on for size in a small town. But I had Terry and his parents and a couple of girlfriends, so I was okay."

"Were you in love with him?"

"With Terry?" she said blankly. "No! I'm sorry if best friends sounds corny, but that's the way it was. Until the night of the first school dance my final year of high school. My mother and I had had a huge fight. She didn't want me going with him—he was the son of a sawyer, after all. She locked me in my room, but I got out through the window and went anyway."

"What floor was your bedroom?"

"I do wish you'd stop interrupting," Marnie said fractiously. "The second floor. Why?"

"Did you jump?"

"I climbed down the Virginia creeper—the stems were thicker than your wrist."

"You really don't like being ordered around, do you?"

"Oh, shush! Anyway, we went to the dance. I had a couple of drinks too many, we drove to the lake to see the moon, and you can guess the rest." She sighed. "Bad mistake, and I'm not just talking about pregnancy, I'm talking about sex. It ruined everything between us—the fun, the friendship. Terry and I avoided each other like the plague for the next few months."

"Was it worth it?" Cal asked softly.

She gaped at him, feeling color creep into her cheeks. "Are you asking if it was good sex? How in the world was I supposed to know? I was sixteen, Cal!"

"You've been with men since then."

She hadn't. But she was darned if that was any of Cal's business. Doggedly, she went on with her story, reciting it as though it had happened to someone else. "I didn't tell my mother I was pregnant. I didn't tell anyone. I wore baggy sweaters and let the waistband of my jeans out and forged a doctor's certificate so I could stay away from gym class.''

"Were you that afraid of her?''

His voice was unreadable. "I was afraid she'd make me have an abortion,'' Marnie said curtly. "So I kept it a secret until it was too late for that. She had tremendous power, Cal. She ran the town. She could give you one look and you'd find yourself doing exactly what she wanted. I hated that! Yes, of course I was afraid of her. Besides, she was as cold as—as the Atlantic Ocean in April.''

"She found out, though.''

"Oh, yes.....'' Marnie's smile was twisted. "Now that was a scene, let me tell you. But in the end she got it out of me that Terry was the father.''

She kicked at the shale with the toe of her sneaker. "I was sent to a private clinic. The town was told I'd gone to a fancy girls' school, and my mother said my cousin Randall from Boston would marry me when the baby was born.'' She talked faster, only wanting done with this. "It was a hard labor, so I was out of it when Kit was born. When I came to, my mother was sitting by the bed. The baby was gone. She'd lied about Randall and the marriage, and she made me sign the consent forms by threatening to fire Terry's father. She'd see he never got another job in the province, that's what she told me. And if I ever tried to trace my child, she'd set a bunch of roughnecks on Terry and his brothers.''

Marnie shivered. "I knew she'd do it. I couldn't risk anything happening to Terry or his family—they were the ones who'd taught me all I ever knew about kindness. So I signed.'' As an afterthought, she added, "My mother also told me I was disinherited. As if that mattered.''

"How did you know your baby was a girl?''

"You sound like a lawyer for the prosecution,'' she

snapped. "One of the cleaning women told me. No one else would say a word, it was as if nothing had ever happened, as if I'd dreamed the whole pregnancy and birth. It was awful. I waited until I felt well enough, then I packed my suitcase and left via the window." She glowered at him. "Ground floor this time. I wrote to my mother two or three times, and after that I wrote every Christmas and for her birthday. But she didn't answer a single one of my letters, and I never saw her again. I found the paper with your name on it in her safe when I went back for the reading of the will. End of story."

"It all sounds so feudal," Cal said.

"So you don't believe me."

"I didn't say that, Marnie."

"You're thinking it."

"You've got to admit it's an incredible story," he said, frowning.

Marnie's mind made an intuitive leap. "You think I've invented all this—straight out of a gothic romance—to cover up my guilt for abandoning my baby."

"Dammit, I don't! I don't know what I think."

Aware of an immense weariness, Marnie said, "It doesn't really matter, does it? The fact is, Kit was adopted, your wife died, and it's in Kit's best interests that I stay out of the picture."

"The fact is," Cal said harshly, "that I don't want you out of the picture. My picture. Despite Kit. Despite common sense and logic and caution. Explain that to me, why don't you? Is that another scene from a gothic romance? I hardly think so."

She folded her arms across her chest. "I don't know what—"

"Don't you, Marnie? Come on, tell the truth."

Her heart was beating in thick, heavy strokes. "No, I don't," she said with a defiant toss of her head.

"Then let me show you."

Cal's footsteps crunched in the shale. His eyes blazing with an emotion she couldn't possibly have categorized, he took her by the shoulders and bent his head. A wave collapsed on the beach in a rattle of stones. The tide's coming up, we should get out of here, Marnie thought foolishly, and felt the first touch of his mouth to hers.

His fingers were digging into her flesh, his lips a hard pressure. Rigid in his embrace, she felt a shudder run through his body. Then gradually his kiss changed, questioning rather than demanding, and his hands left her shoulders, smoothing the rise of her throat and tangling themselves in her hair. Beneath her closed lids, the sun blazed orange.

As abruptly as he'd drawn her to him, Cal pushed her away. Marnie's eyes flew open as he said in a staccato voice, "I shouldn't have done that. Kissing you—Kit's mother—it's the stupidest move I could make."

Marnie asked baldly, "Are you involved with anyone?"

"Are you kidding? In a town the size of Burnham with a twelve-year-old girl in the house? I haven't slept with anyone since my wife died, and why the devil am I telling you something wild horses normally wouldn't drag out of me?"

"I've had exactly one sexual experience in thirty years and that was with Terry."

In sheer disbelief, Cal rasped, "Come off it, Marnie. You don't have to lie to me."

And quite suddenly, Marnie had had enough. The gamut of emotions she'd experienced ever since she'd bumped into a black-haired man in a parking lot in the middle of a thunderstorm now coalesced into pure rage. "I'm sick to death of your disbelieving every word I say!'' she cried, wrenching free of him. ''Let me tell you something, Cal Huntingdon. You think I'd jump in the sack with another man after what happened to me? For nine months I carried my child. That may not sound very long to you because you've had her for almost thirteen years. But to me that was a lifetime. Sure, I was terrified of being found out, and no, I had no idea what I was going to do or whom to turn to. It didn't matter. I loved being pregnant. I felt fiercely protective of my baby and I knew I was going to be the best mother in the whole world.''

She realized through a haze of anger and pain that tears were streaming down her cheeks. Furious with herself for crying, she let her words tumble over each other. ''And then she was taken from me. I never saw her. I had no way of tracing her or getting her back. I've never even known if she was loved.'' Her voice broke. ''How do you think that felt? I've lived with that loss for years, and if you think I was going to risk anything so terrible happening to me again just for the sake of a roll in the hay, you're out of your tree. And I'm *not* crying!''

''Marnie—''

''Go away! Leave me alone. I wish I'd never met you,'' she choked, and swiped at her wet cheeks with the back of her hand.

''It's too late for that,'' Cal said. ''Marnie, don't you see? The story you told me about Kit's birth...the first time, you recited it like something you were reading out of a book, something that never happened to you, and frankly, I found it pretty hard to swallow. But this time, I really heard it. I've seen what it did to you.''

''You mean you believe me?''

He hesitated. ''I'm a lot closer to believing you than I was before.''

"Gee thanks—you're all heart."

"For Pete's sake," he said forcefully, "the past twenty-four hours have thrown me right out of whack. Meeting you in a thunderstorm, your resemblance to Kit, the way I'm pulled to you—I feel like a boxer at the end of the tenth round."

Marnie could relate to this. Again Cal hesitated. "Losing Kit like that, it must have been very difficult—"

"Don't pity me, Cal."

"I'm trying to understand." He gave her a crooked smile. "I wish I'd seen you climbing down the Virginia creeper."

Her breath caught in an undignified hiccup. She said irritably, "I was not wearing a frilly white nightgown. Anyway, gothic heroines have long, raven black hair. That sure lets me out."

Cal said quietly, "You've got hair the color of fire instead."

Had a man ever looked at her quite the way Cal was looking at her now? "You mustn't talk to me like that," she cried.

"I keep telling you I can't help myself!"

Her shoulders slumped. "This has to be the craziest conversation I've ever had in my life," she whispered. "Cal, you're going to drive me back to Burnham right now so I can pick up Christine's car, and then I'm going home. To Faulkner Beach. And I swear, this time I'll stay away from Burnham. I mean it."

"I don't want you to," he burst out. Raking his fingers through his hair, he added in total frustration, "But I haven't got any choice, have I? My first responsibility has to be to Kit. I'm all the security she has. She's so confused, so different from the happy kid she used to be. I'm sure

I'm right in keeping you from her. I've got to be. I can't risk making things any worse than they are.''

''She has to come first,'' Marnie agreed, and found herself smoothing the lines in his cheek, feeling the slight rasp of his beard beneath her fingertips with a primitive thrill of pleasure that made nonsense of her words. She added with patent honesty, ''It won't be as difficult as I thought for me not to see her again...because I know now that she has a good father. One who really loves her.''

Cal's face convulsed with emotion; Marnie's throat tightened as she saw a sheen of tears glitter in his own eyes. He said huskily, ''So you're generous as well as honest. Thanks, Marnie.''

''If I'm honest,'' she said, ''I have to tell you I can't take much more of this. I'm exhausted. Drive me back, Cal, please?''

''Yeah...we'd better get out of here.'' His eyes roamed her face, where the strain of the past couple of hours was only too visible. With an inarticulate groan, he took Marnie in his arms, lowering his head. His lips were warm and by no means as sure of themselves as Marnie might have expected. They spoke to her of a side of him he hadn't put into words, a gentler side that bypassed all her defenses and all the reasons she shouldn't be doing this.

His mouth lingered on hers. Then he explored her cheekbones and her closed lids, his hands stroking her arms from wrist to shoulder. She heard him mutter something against her throat; then once again he kissed her on the lips. A slow heat spread from her belly to her limbs as though the sun were rising within her, bright and warm and beautiful. Her body swayed toward him, her palms pressing to his chest.

She could feel his heart thudding as though he'd run the length of the beach. His kiss deepened, and like a spring flower, Marnie opened to him, exulting in the astonishing intimacy of his tongue on hers. It was like nothing she'd ever felt before, nothing she could possibly have imagined. It was like coming home, she thought, where home was both safety and the wildest of adventures. Her hands slid up the hard, muscled wall of his chest, and linked themselves around his neck, brushing the unexpected silkiness of his hair. As she made a small sound of delight, Cal drew back, his eyes wandering over her dazed features and brilliant sea blue irises. "You're so beautiful you take my breath away," he said thickly, then pulled her the length of his body so they stood hip to hip.

His arousal both excited and terrified her. "Cal, I—"

"Don't tell me you don't want me—I know you do."

"But I'm not—"

Again he closed her lips with his own, his hands traveling the long curve of her spine and the rise of her hips. In a sunburst of longing, Marnie forgot about caution and restraint, those two words that had kept her armored against men ever since Kit was born, and kissed him back with a passionate abandon that made him groan deep in his throat.

Finally, Cal raised his head. His eyes boring into hers, he said roughly, "There's got to be a way out of this, Marnie. I can't just say goodbye to you today, turn my back on you as if you don't exist. I haven't been to bed with anyone since Jennifer died, I told you that. You're the only woman who's made me want to change my mind." He clasped her by the elbows. "You live fifty miles away— that's a safe enough distance. No reason we couldn't have an affair. If it's been thirteen years since you've made love with anyone, you're long overdue. And I know I am."

Marnie stood very still and of all the emotions churning in her belly couldn't have said which was uppermost. Desire? Fury? She said finally, "That would be so easy for you, wouldn't it? Your daughter in Burnham and your mistress in Faulkner. Everything compartmentalized.''

"Easy? No. But I want you...and I need you as my mistress far more than Kit needs you as a mother.''

"No,'' Marnie said.

"What do you mean, no?''

"I mean the opposite of yes,'' she said vigorously. "I don't want to have an affair with anyone. But especially not with you. Cal, you're Kit's father, for heaven's sake!''

"Tell me something I don't know,'' he said sarcastically. "But that's got nothing to do with what's going on between us—you kissed me like there was no tomorrow.''

"Maybe I did. But a kiss is one thing, an affair quite another. I'm not a chess piece made out of ivory that you can move around a board. I've got feelings and a past. Spend a couple of hours a week in bed with you and then the rest of the week pretend you and Kit don't exist? Forget it.''

"You told me you didn't like to play it safe.''

"You're asking me to jump in the deep end of the pool when I can't swim!''

"Sometimes that's the only way to learn!''

"Not for me. The answer's no, Cal, and now would you please drive me back to Burnham?''

"You're making a mistake.''

"An affair would be the mistake.''

His face, she saw distantly, had closed against her, his eyes like stones. "Fine,'' Cal said, then carefully walked around her to climb the bank. As they got in the Cherokee, he said coldly, "You'd better put on your hat and dark glasses.''

As the vehicle jounced through the potholes, Marnie jammed her curls under the brim of her hat and tied the cord ruthlessly tight under her chin. At least her dark glasses hid her from Cal as well as from everyone else in Burnham, she thought, and sat in total silence for the fifteen minutes it took to reach the street with the coffee shop.

Only then did Cal speak. "If you ever need to get in touch with me, I'm head of the university engineering department."

The engineering school at Burnham had one of the finest reputations in the country. So she hadn't been wrong to sense Cal's aura of power. "There's no need for us to keep in touch," she said. "It's too risky."

"I didn't say we'd keep in touch. I meant if there was ever an emergency. Where's your car?"

"It's that white one."

He pulled into the parking space ahead of Christine's Pontiac and said flatly, "Take care of yourself, Marnie."

"I will," Marnie answered with a brittle smile, slid to the sidewalk and slammed the door. Blind to her surroundings, she walked out into the street to get in Christine's car.

She'd lost Kit, found her and lost her again. Whereas Cal—a man different from any other she'd ever met—she'd merely found and lost.

All in less than twenty-four hours.

Dimly, Marnie heard a man yell something from the other side of the road; sunk in her own thoughts, she didn't even bother looking up.

Then everything happened very fast.

The scream of rubber on pavement ripped through the quiet of the little side street. Someone seized her bodily and flung her into the space between the Pontiac and the Cherokee. She banged her hip, her elbow and her cheek on shiny dark green paint. Metal rasped on concrete so close Marnie squeezed her eyes shut; there was a loud clang, followed by several seconds of eerie silence.

"Stay here!" Cal ordered.

Her eyes flew open as he leaped from between the vehicles onto the sidewalk. Slowly, she straightened. So it was Cal who'd grabbed her and thrown her against the Cherokee.

A small blue truck was angled halfway across the sidewalk beyond Christine's car. Its hood was wrapped around a metal pole, which explained the clang. Black skid marks scored the pavement; they'd come within two feet of where she'd been standing.

No wonder Cal had reacted with such speed and violence.

As if it were happening a long way away, Marnie saw Cal open the door of the blue truck and help the driver out: a man in his fifties who was sputtering incoherently about wheels locking and lost steering.

Lost.

Marnie stayed where she was. She hadn't had the time to be frightened beforehand; now she wiped her damp palms down the sides of her jeans and felt her heartbeat racketing in her chest. A police car arrived on the scene. Cal spoke briefly to the officer, then strode back to her. He grasped her by the shoulders. "You okay? Sorry I was so rough, but for the space of five seconds I thought he was going to run you down."

"You sure move fast," Marnie said, rubbing her sore elbow.

He gave her a wolfish grin. "There are some situations where you act first and worry about the consequences afterward."

She gazed at him speculatively. She'd learned a lot about Cal in those few moments. Decisiveness, lightning-swift reflexes, a total disregard for his own safety—he'd displayed them all. And he was still blazing with an energy he was unable to tamp down. ''Did it occur to you that he could've hit you?'' she asked in a neutral voice.

''Nope.''

She added thoughtfully, ''What do you do for excitement, Cal?''

''What do you mean?''

''You're an engineer, a widower, the father of a twelve-year-old. But there's a lot more to you than that.''

''Come off it, Marnie. Anyone else would have shoved you out of the way.''

Others might have tried, but Marnie rather doubted they would have succeeded with as much efficiency and panache as Cal. ''You mentioned something about Third-World guerrillas yesterday—is that where you got your tan?''

''Kit and I went sailing in Tortola on the March break,'' he answered impatiently. ''I didn't hurt you, did I?''

''In other words, mind your own business, Marnie Carstairs.''

''Brains as well as beauty,'' he said with another of those fierce grins.

But Marnie was quite unable to get angry with him. She said soberly, ''Thanks, Cal. You took a terrible risk there.''

''Not really. He didn't even touch your friend's car.''

''You as good as saved my life,'' Marnie said stubbornly.

''You're sure you're all right to drive?''

He wanted to be rid of her; that was the message. If he couldn't take her to bed, he didn't want her at all. Her heart like a boulder in her chest, she said steadfastly, ''Yes, I'm okay. Goodbye, Cal.'' Then she got in Christine's car and drove away from the flashing lights on the police cruiser, from the small crowd that had gathered, and from Cal, who'd risked his life for her and who wanted a tidy, long-distance affair with her.

The whole way home, Marnie forced her attention to her driving, determined not to think about Kit, whom she'd seen so briefly and inconclusively, or to replay all the complexities of the episode with Cal at the picnic table. What had happened there had broken every one of her self-imposed rules. She'd talked about Kit's birth. She'd allowed a man past her defenses.

Bad moves, both of them. Yet had she had a choice?

CHAPTER FIVE

FOR the next few days, Marnie felt as though her sense of time was utterly distorted. Sometimes the minutes crept by so slowly she thought she'd scream—minutes during which she knew she was exiled from her own daughter—and time became an abyss of longing and loss that almost incapacitated her. During these periods, she wished with all her heart that she'd never—from a sense of duty—gone through her mother's papers after her death. Ignorance had been far better than this dull ache that she carried with her everywhere she went.

Her wounds had healed over in the years since she'd given birth; she'd become resigned to her child's absence and been more or less at peace. To discover Kit Huntingdon's existence, so near to her and yet so unutterably far away, had torn all the old scars open so that they were raw and bleeding.

She wasn't sleeping well. She lost weight. Several of her fellow teachers kept asking her what was wrong. Christine was openly worried about her. And to all of them Marnie gave the same safe lies. "I'm fine. Maybe it's a touch of the flu...or spring fever."

But then sometimes she'd be at her desk in the school library or sitting on her deck after work watching the ocean, and she'd realize a whole hour had gone by without her even realizing it, an hour during which she'd gone over in her mind, again and again, every little nuance of that scene in the coffee shop. Every tone of Kit's voice, every implication of her words. Searching for her child. Trying to connect with her the only way she could.

A futile exercise if ever there was one.

Kit was one thing. Cal another.

Marnie thought about him, too, and about his offer of an affair. He haunted her dreams, some of them graphically sexual in a way that made her extremely uneasy. She couldn't afford any breaching of her self-imposed celibacy; she'd been content with it for years. And to end it with Kit's father, of all the men in the world, would be disastrous. Yet Cal's kisses were imprinted on her, body and soul; she couldn't erase them from her memory no matter how hard she tried.

Which didn't stop her from trying.

Unfortunately, it was spring. The sap was rising, the buds were thickening, the birds were mating. Why should she be exempt? Put that together with a man as handsome and sexy as Cal Huntingdon and it spelled trouble. With a capital *T*. Or sex, she thought ruefully, with a capital *S*.

Any number of springs had passed since Kit's birth without her wanting to haul a black-haired man into her bed and throw all her inhibitions out the window. To say yes instead of no.

To once again, metaphorically, take to the Virginia creeper.

Sure, Marnie, and look where that landed you. In the mess you're in now. Forget Cal Huntingdon! Forget he even exists.

As so often happens, that which she was striving to forget forced itself upon her. The first weekend after she'd met Cal, Marnie went rock climbing with her friend Mario on Saturday, and on Sunday she plunged into an orgy of housecleaning; it beat sitting around feeling sorry for herself. She bundled up clothes she no longer wore, scrubbed the kitchen cupboards and cleaned the oven, then went through all her books, sorting out a pile she'd take to the secondhand bookshops in Halifax. When she was halfway through a pile of magazines, a headline across the cover leaped out at her. Engineer With A Difference, it said.

She flipped the magazine open and turned to the article. With a strange sense of fatality—did she really think she was going to escape him?—she found herself staring at a photo montage of Cal. Cal wearing a summer-weight suit, posed with a group of officials in Ghana. Cal naked to the waist beside a new water-purifying system in southern India. Cal in steel-toed boots and dirty khaki pants supervising the construction of an eye clinic in Bangladesh.

Her housecleaning forgotten, Marnie hunkered down on the floor and started to read. Fifteen minutes later, she was sitting staring into space. Cal's other commitment, besides being head of the engineering school, was as a consulting engineer to various charitable organizations on a strictly volunteer basis. So this was what he'd meant by travel.

The magazine was dated two and a half years ago. Before Jennifer died.

Oh, damn, Marnie thought helplessly. Damn and double damn. Why do I have to find out Cal's everything I admire? A man who takes risks. A man who cares about other people and puts his life on the line to show that he cares. Because one thing the article made clear was that Cal had, on occasion, found himself face-to-face with rebels who didn't appreciate his humanitarian acts, as well as with regimes who'd rather he went elsewhere. Face-to-face with danger. Very real danger.

This was where he'd honed his reflexes, the alertness to threat and disregard for his own safety that he'd demonstrated on that side street in Burnham, and where he'd met up with the guerrillas he'd mentioned. She'd been right to guess there was more to him than showed on the surface. A great deal more.

She had no recollection of ever having read the article before. But then she often canceled her magazine subscriptions because she never seemed to get around to reading them.

Marnie put the magazine to one side and went into the kitchen to make a cup of tea. And that night she dreamed about Cal again.

Two days after Marnie had read the article about Cal, she stayed in school after hours. The Compton Junior High Cougars were to play her own school's basketball team; the finals were just getting under way. Marnie's duties included providing a canteen during the game and hot dogs afterward. She liked doing this. One reason she'd become a teacher was to keep in touch with kids.

She hurried down the corridor carrying an armload of wiener buns. Ketchup, mustard and relish were next on the list, and she mustn't forget to check the cooler. By the time she got to the canteen, a couple of the visiting players were waiting for her. With a frown of puzzlement, she realized they weren't wearing the red-and-green uniforms of the Cougars.

Across the blue singlet of the nearer girl was inscribed Burnham Bears. Marnie dropped the buns in an untidy heap on the counter and said faintly, "What are you doing here? Your team doesn't even belong to our league."

"Yep," one of the girls said, "we do now. There was a big shuffle a couple days ago."

The other girl said, "Wow, you sure look like one of our forwards. I was just reading about movie look-alikes...that's cool. C'n I have a bag of dill chips?"

"Yes," Marnie said. Clamping down on a terror that could easily reduce her to a blithering idiot, she opened the cash box and somehow counted out the right change. Then she locked the cash in a drawer and hurried back down the corridor toward the staff room. She'd get on the phone. Christine would spell her. And she'd get out of here as fast as she could.

As she rounded the corner, she nearly collided with another Burnham player. Horrified, she saw it was Kit's friend, Lizzie. Wishing the floor would open to engulf her, she ducked her head and almost leaped away from the girl. But Lizzie was gaping at her as if she'd never seen a teacher before.

"Hey!" Lizzie cried. "You look just like—who *are* you?"

Ironically, it was the identical question Cal had asked. "Sorry, I'm in a hurry," Marnie mumbled, and fled down the corridor. The staff room, thank goodness, was empty. With shaking fingers, she punched in Christine's number.

No answer.

She then tried two other teachers. One wasn't home, the other had a migraine. Very slowly, Marnie put down the receiver and looked up the number for the School of Engineering at Burnham University. A businesslike secretary connected her to Cal's extension. It rang once. Then his voice, horribly familiar, announced that he had left the office for the day and would return her call the next morning, please leave a message at the sound of the beep.

What was the good of that? Tomorrow morning was far too late. With a moan of dismay, Marnie clunked the receiver back into its cradle and realized she was wringing her hands in true gothic style.

Okay, okay, she told herself, calm down. Think. It's time for some damage control. You'll go straight to the Faulkner coach and plead a migraine even though you've never had one in your life, and then you'll go out the back door and run home as if all the demons in hell are after you.

Kit won't see you. And Lizzie, providing she doesn't run into you again, can't do any lasting harm. So she's seen someone who resembles Kit. So what?

Her heart began to feel as though it might stay confined by her rib cage, although a light tremor still shook her fingers. On impulse, Marnie dialed one more teacher, discovering to her great relief that he could come in half an hour. She glanced at her watch. The game would begin in fifteen minutes. Everything was going to be all right.

Marnie stood up, wriggling her shoulders and rotating her neck in an attempt to relax. Then she got up and opened the staff-room door.

Kit and Lizzie were standing outside in the corridor.

Lizzie looked excited, Kit terrified. Marnie put on her most schoolmarmish expression and said briskly, "If you need a phone, you can use the one down the hall." Giving them a brief nod, she started to walk past them.

In a voice that quivered with strain, Kit said, "You look just like me."

For the first time in her life, Marnie looked her daughter full in the face and, with an enormous effort, kept her own face expressionless. In the same cool tone she said, "I suppose I do a bit. Although your eyes are a different color and your hair's redder than mine. You must excuse me, I have to—"

"Are you my mother?" Kit gasped. "My real mother?"

Marnie's face muscles felt as though they had congealed; an actual headache began to throb through her temples. Although each word felt like a repudiation of her very soul, she said stiffly, "I have no idea what you're talking about.

The game's nearly due to start. Shouldn't you both be in the gym?''

''You've got to be my mother,'' Kit said, her words falling all over each other. ''I don't care what you say, you look so much like me. I'm adopted, you see. My parents told me when I was very young, and until my mother died...'' Briefly, she stumbled. ''Not my—my biological mother. My other mother. Anyway, she died. The past couple of months, I've been asking my dad about my real mother, wanting to find out about her...about you. He hates it when I do that, but I have to, don't you see? I have to know! And then Lizzie told me about bumping into you and so we've been looking for you everywhere.''

Marnie stood very still. Her brain cells seemed to have stopped working. She even felt as though her blood had coagulated in her veins. On top of meeting Kit under the very worst of circumstances, she now knew that once more Cal hadn't been honest with her. He'd never mentioned that Kit had evinced an interest in her biological mother—information that was surely crucial to Marnie. How could he have been so deceitful? So cruel?

Taking a deep breath, Marnie made one more valiant attempt. ''I'm sorry,'' she said gently, ''I can see how important this is to you. But just because you want to find your—your real mother, you can't go around inventing her...as you're doing now.'' She gave Kit the best smile she could muster. ''Good luck with your game.''

She shouldn't have smiled. Kit said frantically, ''When you smile, your front teeth are crooked just the same way as mine. I'm not making this up. You *are* my mother, I know you are!''

Her voice had risen and her brown eyes were wide with pain. Desperate to comfort her, Marnie made her second mistake. ''Kit—'' she blurted.

"You know my name! How do you know my name?"
Because your father told me. "I heard your friend—"

"I never mentioned Kit's name," Lizzie said triumphantly. Lizzie was clearly enjoying all this drama.

In a wild flood of words, Kit accused, "You didn't want me when I was born and you don't want me now! How could you have abandoned me? Was I so awful you didn't love me even a little bit?"

"I—"

"My mother died and left me, and now you're just the same. I hate you both! You don't even have the guts to say I'm your daughter, not even after I've stayed out of your way for nearly thirteen years. I hate you, do you hear me? I *hate* you!"

Tears were dripping from Kit's cheeks onto her singlet. Marnie said decisively, "Kit, stop it. You know nothing about me or the circumstances that—"

"I know you just lied to me. Told me I'd invented you. Called me by name when you shouldn't have known my name."

As forcefully as she could, Marnie said, "My own mother only died a month ago. Until then I never knew who'd adopted you."

"Save your excuses for someone dumb enough to believe them," Kit flung. "I don't want to hear them. It's too late, don't you see? Or are you stupid as well as a liar?"

Lizzie drew in her breath in a fascinated gasp. Marnie could have said, "Your father doesn't want you to know about me." It would have been true. But somehow, even though Cal had lied to her, she found she couldn't say those particular words. On the other hand, she wasn't going to let Kit walk all over her. "Please, Kit, if I lied, it was for the best of reasons," she said.

"Sure. So you don't have to stop and look at the way

you behaved," Kit cried. "All mothers are supposed to love their kids. But not you, you're different. You never loved me. Well, that's fine with me. If you don't want me, then I don't want you. I never want to see you again. Never, do you hear me? Never in my whole life!"

Marnie had been convinced when she'd recovered consciousness in the clinic and found her mother sitting by the bed that she couldn't ever again feel pain to compare with the emptiness of her arms...empty of her child. But now, in a school corridor many years later, she was being proven wrong. Her daughter hated her. Was repudiating her.

White-faced, Marnie stood very still, Kit's words echoing in her brain. Her tongue was frozen to the floor of her mouth; her limbs felt like blocks of ice. And then, from the corner of her eye she saw a flicker of movement. A man was standing in the corridor behind Kit. A black-haired man. Cal.

He must have heard every word his daughter had said.

This has got to be a nightmare, she thought crazily. In a few moments, the alarm will ring and I'll wake up and get ready for school. Please, God, let it be a nightmare.

Cal said flatly, "Kit, I'll take you home."

Kit whirled. "Dad!" Her breath caught in a sob. "Oh, Dad...I'm so glad to see you," she cried, and ran to him, throwing her arms around him and burying her face in his chest.

He was wearing a shirt and tie along with a sport jacket. At any other time, Marnie might have noticed how handsome he looked. But all she was aware of was how naturally Kit had sought his embrace. I'm jealous, she thought blankly.

She said in a voice that didn't sound remotely like her own, "Cal, what are you doing here?"

"Kit left a note on the kitchen table telling me the team

was coming to Faulkner. I saw it as soon as I got home from work.'' He looked Marnie up and down. ''You didn't expect me to turn up, did you?''

''You think I *planned* this?'' Marnie croaked. ''That it was a setup?''

''You're the school librarian and school got out over an hour ago. So why are you still here?''

Blessedly, a lick of fire began to melt the ice in which Marnie felt encased. She was damned if she was going to plead her case. Why bother? Cal had already condemned her. She said bitterly, ''Why didn't you tell me that for the past couple of months Kit has been asking about me? About her biological mother? All your lies are by omission, aren't they?''

Kit had raised her head, her face tear streaked, and was looking from one to the other. ''You know about her, Dad?''

Cal said. ''We met by chance ten days ago in Burnham. I told her to stay away from you.''

Kit's face crumpled. ''I want to go home,'' she whispered.

He curved his arm around her. ''That's exactly where we're going, hon.''

Two against one, Marnie thought with painful accuracy. And she, Marnie, was the one left out. Alone. The way she'd always been, even when she lived with her mother.

Cal was speaking again. ''Lizzie,'' he said, ''I want you to go to the coach and tell him Kit isn't feeling well and I'm taking her home. Please don't tell anyone what happened here today. I know I can trust you.'' Then he shifted his gaze to Marnie, his eyes as hard as flint. ''Maybe you could do us all a favor and go home, too—before any more damage is done.''

Her head high, Marnie looked him straight in the eye

and said, "Ever since I found out half an hour ago that Burnham was playing here today, I've done my very best to avoid this situation. If you choose to think the worst of me, that's your problem."

He didn't say a word. Turning on his heel, he led Kit away, his arm around his daughter's waist.

His daughter. Not hers.

Lizzie had vanished, too. Very slowly, Marnie walked the other way down the hall, toward the canteen. The game would have started by now. She'd get everything ready for the break and go home.

By now, her headache was all too real. Served her right, she thought wretchedly, wrote a note about the workings of the steamer, the grill and the cash box, then left the school.

Once she was home, Marnie took a couple of Tylenol, fell instantly asleep and woke five hours later from a nightmare in which Cal was chasing her around the basketball court with a cleaver, Kit and Lizzie cheering him on. The two girls were dressed up like blue grizzly bears.

It was pitch-dark. She could hear the fall of waves on the beach; a car swished past, its headlights briefly reflected in the mirror over the dresser. Her headache seemed to have gone. But none of the drug companies had invented a pill for heartache, she thought, and felt the first slow tears seep down her cheeks.

CHAPTER SIX

THE next day, Marnie and Christine shared yard duty at morning recess. The sun was shining and a playful wind was blowing from the sea; at any other time Marnie would have been happy to be outdoors. But not today. Today, the only thing that could make her happy would be to have Kit run into her arms as yesterday she'd run into Cal's: with the complete naturalness of someone who knows where she belongs.

No hope of that, thought Marnie, and gave Christine a smile she did her best to make convincing. Christine, however, took one look at Marnie's face and said, "You're coming to my house right after school, I'll feed you fish chowder, and you're going to tell me what's gone wrong the past couple of weeks." As Marnie opened her mouth, Christine added fiercely, "And don't argue. I've kept my distance for days, figuring you'd tell me what was up when you were ready. I'm not waiting any longer."

Yesterday, after Cal and Kit had left the school, Marnie had felt cripplingly alone, but she didn't have to feel alone with Christine today. "All right," she said meekly.

"Good," Christine said, the breeze disarranging her sleek brown hair. "Now I'd better go and stop Billie Shipley from peddling cigarettes on the school grounds. Does he think I'm blind?"

"Hey, at least it's not hash," Marnie said, her smile more genuine, and with affection watched her friend stride away. Christine was engaged to the local doctor; she was a loyal and fun-loving friend.

66

She was also a dedicated gardener and an atrocious housekeeper. At four-thirty, Marnie cleared a laundry basket full of crumpled towels from the nearest chair, deposited them on the dining-room table next to a pile of English exams and accepted a glass of Chardonnay in an elegant crystal glass that wasn't quite as clean as it should be.

Oh, well, she thought, alcohol kills germs, and raised her glass. "To your garden."

"Raccoons dug up half my tulips. So I'm going to drink to you instead. May you look like a human being again soon. Cheers."

Wryly, Marnie took a sip. It was, as she'd expected, an excellent wine, dry with just a hint of fruitiness. Before she could think of what to say next, Christine's cat launched itself onto the table; some of the exams slid to the floor.

"Good place for them," Christine said gloomily. "I sometimes wonder if any of my students hear one word I say." The vagaries of adolescents were a safe enough topic. Marnie latched onto it with relief. But as soon as she paused for breath, Christine said, "Can it, Marnie. What's up?"

Marnie looked at her in silence. When she'd taken the job in Faulkner, she and Christine had hit it off right away and become the best of friends. Last year, Christine had been careful not to let her growing romance with Don, the doctor, harm the friendship. Such concern, Marnie knew, was far more important than piles of dirty towels. And if she hadn't been prepared to tell all, she'd have turned down Christine's invitation...wouldn't she?

She said uncertainly, "Chris, only two other people know what I'm going to tell you. One of them lives in Australia and the other in Burnham, and it's essential this remain between you and me. You wouldn't believe what a mess I'm in."

"Give," Christine said.

So Marnie did. Slowly at first, then more rapidly as she lost herself in the story, she told Christine about her mother and Terry and the school dance; about the clinic and the adoption of her child. "I ran away a week after she was born, worked my butt off to get my arts and library degrees, then got my first job here three years ago September," she said. Then she told about meeting Cal in the parking lot and everything that had ensued after that, even including Cal's offer of a long-distance affair. She finished with the nasty scene in the school corridor before the basketball game. "I haven't heard from either one of them since then, nor do I expect to," she concluded, and took another big mouthful of wine.

Christine had paid her the compliment of complete silence during her recital. Now she said, "But Cal can't go around pretending you don't exist. And Kit will want to see you again once she gets over the shock."

"I don't think so."

"It isn't over," Chris said forcefully. "It can't be."

"She hates me, and he thinks I deceived him. I'd say it's over."

"You've got to fight for her!"

"How?" Marnie demanded. "Ring the front doorbell and say I've come for tea? Kit thinks I've abandoned her twice now—thirteen years ago as well as outside the staff room. She's an adolescent. We both know they're not the most rational of creatures. Plus Cal doesn't want me coming anywhere near her. As if I had some kind of disgusting disease. Pour me some more wine. Maybe if I get royally sloshed, I'll feel better."

"No way. We've got to keep our heads here."

"Do you think I haven't stayed awake night after night trying to figure a way out of this mess?" Marnie cried.

"There's only one thing I can do. Next week when the transfers come in, I'm going to ask for a school at the very tip of Cape Breton. That's about as far away as I can get from Burnham and still be in Nova Scotia."

"You're going to run away?" Christine squeaked.

"You're darn right I am."

"You can't," Chris wailed. "She's your daughter!"

In a low voice, Marnie said, "I know that, Chris."

"Oh, Marnie, I'm sorry. I'm not handling this well at all." Christine plunked her glass down and gave Marnie a clumsy hug. "You've got to admit it's been rather a shock. Although it does explain why you run a country mile any time a man gets the slightest bit interested in you."

"I'll never risk getting hurt like that again."

"That might have been true before you met Kit and Cal. But it's too late now. You have met them—and you're hurting anyway. Hurting bad." Christine paused, her head to one side, and asked with genuine interest, "What does Cal look like?"

"Oh, he's a hunk," Marnie said wearily. "So what?"

"Hmm… Marnie, there's got to be something I can do to help."

"Pray for a librarian's post in northern Cape Breton."

"I'm certainly not going to do that!"

"There's nothing you can do," Marnie said. "But thanks for listening…and now I'd really love some of that fish chowder, Chris. For the first time in days, I feel hungry."

After supper, they walked over to Don's place and the three of them went for a long walk on the beach. When Marnie got home, she fell into bed and slept soundly without a single nightmare.

She was glad she'd told Christine. It couldn't change either Kit or Cal or the heartache that was her constant companion, but it did make her feel less alone.

Her mother had cut herself off from intimacy. Marnie didn't want to be like her mother.

Several days went by. The first leaves came out on the trees, vibrantly green. Christine and Marnie made rhubarb chutney; on the weekend, Marnie went white-water canoeing. The days were getting longer and the heat of the sun more convincing.

Despite Christine's best efforts at cheering her up, Marnie carried an ache of loss with her wherever she went: that Kit should be so close to her geographically and so far emotionally was like a form of unremitting torture. She endured it because she had to. But she didn't regain the weight she'd lost, and her eyes had a haunted look she couldn't seem to banish.

She tried very hard not to think about Cal at all but failed miserably. In three meetings, all of which had been fraught with emotion, he'd forced himself into her life, awakening sexual longings that had slumbered for years, as well as other needs less tangible, although equally unsettling. The need for love? she found herself wondering. Surely not.

She did her best to stifle all these longings. On the first really hot day of the year, when it seemed as though all the students in the school had made a pact to be uncooperative, Marnie went straight home at four o'clock, changed her clothes and went down to the beach below her house with her neighbor's black Labrador retriever. A game of fetch ensued, during which both of them got very wet and Marnie laughed a lot. Maybe Midnight was laughing, too, she thought, amused by the dog's gaping jaws and thrashing tail.

She threw the rubber ball out into the sea again, watching Midnight buck the waves. Then behind her, Marnie heard the crunch of footsteps on the loose stones above the sand. Expecting it to be her neighbor, she turned with a smile.

Her jaw dropped. "Cal!"

He was wearing beige cotton trousers with a short-sleeved white shirt, his tie loosened; his eyes were watchful. Like a hunter's eyes, Marnie thought fancifully, and shivered from more than the icy shock of a wave over her bare toes. Then she noticed something else: how grim he looked, how he wasn't making even a pretense of smiling.

In sudden terror, the color draining from her face, she stammered, "K-Kit...something's happened to Kit." Why else would he have sought her out? The sand lurched under her feet. She never fainted, she thought fuzzily. She couldn't start now.

In a blur of movement, Cal was at her side, grabbing her around the waist. "Kit's fine. Nothing's happened to her. I'm sorry, Marnie, I didn't mean to scare you."

As she sagged in his hold, Midnight raced up the sand, dropped the ball and shook himself, showering them both with cold water. Marnie took a couple of steadying breaths, her head settling back on her shoulders where it belonged, and heard Cal ask, "Is that your dog?"

With Cal's arrival, the zest had gone from the game and all the hurt of the past few days had resurfaced. Marnie said, "No, it's not. I don't want you here, Cal. We've got nothing to say to each other."

"I wouldn't be here if that was true."

"I'm not going to have an affair with you, I've stayed away from Kit and now I'm going home. I wish you'd do the same."

Marnie marched up the beach, aware through every nerve ending in her body of Cal close behind her. After she crossed the shoal of stones, she sent Midnight home along the path that joined the two properties. Then she padded through the spruce trees behind her house.

When she opened the screen door, Cal followed her inside. She turned to face him, folding her arms across her chest, wishing she was wearing anything but the briefest of shorts and an old fuschia shirt whose tails she'd tied under her breasts and whose color clashed violently with her hair. Each word like a shard of glass, she said, "How did you find out where I live?"

His smile was ironic. "Following your example, I asked at the local gas station."

"Very funny. Do you make a practice of invading people's privacy like this?"

"Knock it off, Marnie. I didn't bother phoning ahead of time because I was nine-tenths sure you'd slam the receiver in my ear," he said. "Why don't you go change? You're cold. Then we'll talk."

"I don't want to talk to you, so why don't you leave? And don't bother coming back."

Thrusting his hands into his pockets, he said, "I've come to eat crow. Which will no doubt make you laugh yourself silly. But I'm not going to start groveling until you've changed. Right now, instead of focusing on Kit and what's going on at home—why I'm here, in other words—all I can see is how long your legs are in those goddamned shorts. They aren't even decent, for Pete's sake."

Her shorts had shrunk in the drier. She tugged at the hem. "So am I supposed to feel flattered?"

"I don't give a damn whether you're flattered or not! All I know is that when I look at you in that getup, I want to haul you to the nearest bedroom and make love to you until neither one of us has the energy to stand up, let alone talk about Kit. And what kind of father does that make me?'' He swung around, staring moodily out to sea through the big window. "Go change. Please.''

He looked, she thought with unwilling compassion, like a man at the end of his rope. "Is this your standard approach to women? You won't win any prizes for subtlety, I'll tell you that.''

"The one way I don't feel around you is subtle. For God's sake, Marnie, will you go change?''

The rebellion Charlotte Carstairs had never fully quelled in Marnie flared into life. Instead of running for her bedroom, locking the door and changing into her most unbecoming outfit, preferably something black that swathed her from throat to ankle, she announced, "I'll never understand men, not if I live to be ninety. You don't like me or trust me or respect me and yet you say you want to make love to me." Bitterness spilled into her voice. "You're not interested in making love, Cal. It's all the other words, the cheap four-letter ones, that's what you want.''

He stepped closer; he could move very quickly for so big a man. "I want you in my bed, that's what I want, and quite frankly I don't care what words we use.''

It was not the right moment for Marnie to remember some of the things she and Cal had done in her dreams. She said coldly, "I already said no. And the way you and Kit behaved at the school has given me no incentive to change my mind.''

He said stiffly, "I came here—among other reasons—to apologize for that." For a moment, he glanced through the window at the restless, sparkling ocean. Then he said hoarsely, "The way you kissed me at the picnic spot—were you just faking it? Was I way off base to think you wanted me as much as I wanted you?''

Marnie flushed, her mind skittering among a variety of replies ranging from truthful to downright lies. Then Cal added with savage emphasis, "I know as Kit's father I haven't got the right to ask you that. But I need to know— it's important."

She had no idea what he was getting at. "I've got a question for you first," she said evenly, "a very obvious question, I suppose. Did you love your wife, Cal?"

His fists clenched at his sides. "Yes." As though the words were being dragged from him, he said, "Watching her die, feeling so helpless—it was the hardest thing I've ever done."

No wonder he'd suggested a long-distance affair, Marnie thought reluctantly. He didn't want Marnie encroaching in any way on his life with Jennifer. This realization hurt rather more than she was willing to admit; but it did help her understand Cal a little better. She said quietly, "When you kissed me, I wasn't faking anything."

His breath escaped in a small whoosh. "Come here," he said.

"Cal, neither of us should—"

He rested a fingertip on her lips, then bent his head to kiss her, his hands resting on her shoulders. It was a long, exploratory kiss, his tongue dancing with hers, his mouth traveling the line of her throat to the hammering pulse at its base. He murmured, "You taste of salt," and kissed her full on the lips again, deeply and passionately, taking Marnie to a place she'd never been before, a place where sunlight glinted on white foam and waves of longing surged through her body. Unconsciously, she swayed toward him, feeling the tautness of his chest brush her breasts. Her nipples hardened under her thin shirt, and for the first time in days, she forgot about Kit and the pain of loss. This kiss wasn't about loss. It was about discovery and wonderment.

Roughly, Cal put his arms around her, drawing her to the length of his body so that she felt, unmistakably, the hardness of his erection. The shock ran through her body. Wary as a wild creature, she raised her head, in her eyes a mingling of passion and panic. "Cal, we mustn't! Don't you see? Kit'll always be between us and—"

"You think I don't know that?" he muttered, and kissed her again.

She was drowning, she thought confusedly, drowning in the throb of blood through her veins and the fierce impulsion to know more. Of what use caution when Cal's hands were cupping her face, his lips searching the softness of her own, his body heat warming that place deep inside where no one had ever reached her before? In one kiss, Cal was teaching her something that Terry, in his awkward lovemaking by the lake, hadn't even known.

But Terry's lovemaking had given her Kit.

Marnie dragged her head free and struck away Cal's hands. "Stop it! Oh, God, what am I doing? I must be out of my mind."

She was trembling, her expression distraught. Cal said urgently, "Don't tell me it's wrong, what we're doing—it can't be. Not when we both feel—"

"Cal, Terry and I were together just once and I got pregnant. Are you planning a repeat? Is that why you're here? To make a little sister or brother for Kit?"

"Don't be ridiculous! When you and I make love, we'll use protection. Do you think I'm totally irresponsible?"

"*When* we make love? You're very sure of yourself!"

In one searing glance, he traveled her body from head to foot, missing, she was sure, not one detail of her tangled hair, her flushed cheeks and heightened breathing, the thrust of her breasts against her shirt and the slim length of her legs, bared by the skimpy shorts. Then he looked straight at her, his eyes boring into hers. "Yeah, I came here today to talk about Kit. That's true enough and it's extremely important. But there was another reason I came. I couldn't stay away. Even though I know I'm a fool for being here, I had to see you again.''

"You've seen me," she said stonily. "Now you can go home. Because all you want from me is sex."

"And what's wrong with that? It's been two years, Marnie!"

"There must be a dozen women between here and Burnham—not one of them related to Kit—who'd be delighted to go to bed with you. But I'm not available. Please—just go home and leave me alone."

"I'm not going anywhere until we sit down like two reasonable adults and discuss my daughter. Who also happens to be your daughter."

"So what were you doing? Softening me up with a few kisses first?" she taunted, and watched him flinch as though she'd struck him. "Oh, hell and damnation," she muttered, "I turn into the prize bitch of the year when I'm around you. I'm going to get changed."

Marnie shut the door to her bedroom with a decisive snap and stared blindly at the clothes in her closet. She shouldn't have accused Cal of an ulterior motive when he'd kissed her. She was no expert, but she'd swear those kisses hadn't been fake, any more than her own. He had, she was almost sure, been speaking the truth when he'd said he couldn't stay away from her.

And how he hated that.

Absently, Marnie ran her fingers along the row of hangers. The truth was achingly simple. Cal desired her. But he loved Jennifer, who to all intents and purposes had been Kit's mother.

With a jagged sigh, she changed into a pair of cotton trousers and a loose green shirt, jamming her bare feet into socks. Then she brushed her hair and pulled it back into a ponytail. She didn't put on lipstick or earrings.

Let him see her as she was.

Taking a deep breath, she opened the door and walked back into the living room.

CHAPTER SEVEN

CAL was standing by the bookshelves, holding a framed
photograph in his hand. He said harshly, "Is this Kit's father?"

If she'd known Cal was coming, Marnie would have put
away that particular photograph. She walked over to him,
glancing down at the picture. "Yes. Her father and her
grandparents."

The photo had been taken when Marnie was sixteen,
shortly before the school dance; she was laughing into the
camera, one arm around Terry, the other around Marylou,
his mother. His dad, Dave, was also hugging Marylou.
They all looked very happy.

"Where do they live now?" Cal asked.

"Marylou and Dave still live in the same house in
Conway Mills. Dave's retired. He used to work in the mill.
Terry left there as soon as he graduated from high school.
He studied commerce and got involved in international
banking. He lives in Australia. He was back in Canada four
or five years ago for a conference, and that's when I told
him about the baby he'd fathered. I felt he had to know—
I should've told him long before."

"He's a good-looking guy. So you're still in touch with
him?"

"He phones out of the blue at all sorts of weird hours
from places like Kyoto and Kuala Lumpur—he's always
hated writing letters. He hasn't told his parents about the
baby, and neither have I. What was the point?"

Restlessly, Cal put the photo down, looking around him.
It was a small room, welcoming yet unpretentious, the walls
painted white, the wooden floor blue, clusters of scarlet

geraniums in pots by the picture window that overlooked the ocean. "Lots of travel posters," he commented. "You've been around. Did you like Costa Rica?"

"Cal, those are all the places I want to go. Not the places I've been to."

He raised one brow. "Teachers earn good money. You could afford to travel."

She said sharply, "Am I on trial again?"

"That heap outside your door you call a car—it doesn't even look safe."

"It nearly always gets me where I want to go."

"Do you own this house?"

"I rent it."

Again he looked around. All her furniture was obviously secondhand, yet carefully refurbished. "The paintings," he said in a neutral voice. "Who did those?"

"Me."

He walked over to one of them. They were all abstracts, swirls of bright colors infused with energy and abandon. He said with a genuine smile, "I like them—they're very like you."

"Ever since I saw an article in the newspaper about that painting that was nothing but a few vertical stripes and the National Gallery paid a million dollars for it, I figured I could paint, too." Her smile was mischievous. "Sometimes I do stripes. But mostly I do blobs."

"Nonrepresentational postmodernism," he said solemnly.

"So how come nobody's offering *me* a million dollars?"

"Don't quit your day job." Cal chuckled, adding spontaneously, "I like the way you can laugh at yourself, Marnie—you'd be surprised how few people can do that."

"I don't think you laugh enough. At anything."

He said dryly, "You haven't exactly been seeing me at my best. One of these days we should try something like a normal date. You know the kind of thing—pizza and a movie.''

She didn't think that was very likely; nor was she about to tell Cal that when he did laugh she wanted to throw herself at him regardless of the consequences. Why had she never realized how sexy a man's laugh could be? She said casually, "You came here, I believe, to eat crow. Or so you said. Would you like coffee or a beer to wash it down?''

He yanked at his tie, tossing it over the back of the wooden rocking chair. "A beer'd be great," he said, and followed her into the tiny kitchen, his eyes, she saw, not missing one detail.

To her dismay, he walked straight over to the two photos hanging by the sink. In one, a red-haired woman was bracing her canoe in the rapids of a rock-strewn river; in the other, the same woman was gripping a cliff face, the edge of rock and sky a knife-sharp line.

Bending forward to see them better, Cal said, "That's you.''

Marnie would have moved those photos, too, had she known he was coming. "Mmm...I told you I don't like to play it safe.''

"Rephrase that. You like to play it dangerous.''

There was a note in his voice she couldn't decipher. "You've got a problem with that?''

"I used to do white-water kayaking and deep-sea diving before I got married...but never rock climbing. I'm terrified of heights. Why do you flirt with danger, Marnie?''

"So I won't end up like my mother," she said flippantly. "Better to love danger than power.''

"Yet for thirteen years you've stayed away from men. So you told me.''

He'd cut to the heart of it. She said in an unfriendly voice, "Yeah...aren't you the clever one?'' and reached into the refrigerator for the beer.

''And why no travel and a wreck of a car and a rented house not big enough to swing a skunk in?''

Marnie uncapped the beer and took out a glass, plunking both down on the counter, her nostrils flaring. ''You're like the Grand Inquisitor! Let me ask you something, for a change. You've got money. I saw your house, I know the cost of waterfront properties in towns like Burnham. How can you afford that on a university salary?''

''My parents and Jennifer's both had money,'' he said.

Nothing in his voice had changed, but Marnie had never been insensitive to implication. ''I suppose you inherited Jennifer's share. I'm sorry, I didn't mean to be unkind. But, Cal, I left home at seventeen. I stole money for bus fare from my mother's wallet the day Kit was born and I pawned my grandmother's diamond ring to pay the rent on my first apartment. I got jobs in restaurants and grocery stores to put myself through university because I have this little problem—I like to eat. I'm still paying off my student loans, and until I'm debt-free, I'm not traveling anywhere or buying a house or a new car.'' Her smile was full of self-mockery. ''However, I do own my own canoe and my rock-climbing equipment—all top of the line.''

''When your mother died—didn't you get anything?''

She gazed out the window at the phalanx of spruce trees. ''She left me one hundred dollars.''

''So she never forgave you.''

''I guess not.'' Abruptly, Marnie reached up and hauled the band from her ponytail, shaking her hair free in a rich cloud around her head. ''I never want to be like her,'' she said violently. ''Mean of spirit. Isolated from other people.''

''Marnie,'' Cal said, amusement threading his voice, ''I don't think you have to worry.''

''Don't laugh at me!''

''I'm not. I don't know you well, but anyone who can work with adolescents all day isn't what you'd call isolated.

And there's not even a hint of meanness in you. Or in your blobs, for that matter."

Suddenly, her eyes were dancing. "But what about the stripes?"

"The vertical ones? Oh, that's easy. Sexual sublimation," he said blandly.

She blushed. "We're a long way from the subject of crow, Cal Huntingdon."

"We were talking about money. Your lack of it." His smile faded. "Terry's an international banker and he won't even help you out?"

"He offered. I refused."

"It seems Kit comes by her stubbornness honestly."

"Drink your beer," Marnie said crossly.

"Let's get something straight first—you're not on trial, Marnie. But I've got this hunger to know everything about you and I'm doing a lousy job hiding that." He added forcefully, "Even in a shirt six sizes too big for you, you're so beautiful you take my breath away."

She said faintly, "I think I'd better have a beer, too."

With sudden urgency, Cal added, "Would you go to bed with me? Or am I fooling myself?"

"How can I answer that?" Marnie cried. "We scarcely know each other and all we do is argue, and then there's Kit. We can't pretend she's not a major factor in all this."

"Yes or no. That's how you answer it."

"I just don't know. I keep telling you I don't let men anywhere near me. Men make babies—surely I don't have to spell that out." Infinitesimally, his face altered. In swift compunction, Marnie said, "I've done it again, haven't I? Hurt you. I'm sorry, Cal. You and Jennifer…why did you adopt a baby? Why didn't you have your own?"

"A year after we married, Jennifer got cancer of the uterus," he said in a clipped voice. "She had to have a hysterectomy. She was devastated. She really wanted a family. We started making inquiries about adoption, and when we got the call from the clinic, we adopted Kit.''

Marnie said slowly, ''And what about you? You loved Jennifer. But married to her, you could never father your own child.''

''As you should know better than most, life doesn't always work out the way you want it to.''

''Is that why you went overseas so much?'' she asked even more slowly. ''Another sort of sublimation?''

He rapped, ''How do you know about that?''

''I saw an article about you in a magazine.''

''I sure wish you'd quit prying.''

''So you want to know everything about me, but I'm not supposed to know anything about you?''

''I'm not used to talking about myself,'' Cal said.

''You got that right,'' Marnie said sardonically. ''If all women are afraid of thunder, all men are afraid of showing their feelings.''

''How would you know?'' he said nastily. ''You don't have anything to do with men.''

''I have several male friends, married and unmarried. I just don't go around kissing them or getting into bed with them.''

Deliberately, Cal smoothed the line of her shoulders through her shirt, then ran his fingers through her hair; his face was very close to hers. His lashes, she noticed abstractedly, were thicker than hers. He said, ''I plan to be the exception to that rule.''

''Huh,'' Marnie said.

''But in the meantime, have you got anything I can nibble on—besides you? I didn't have time for lunch today.''

He was like a whirlwind, Marnie thought, picking her up, swirling her around, then putting her down somewhere else. She said, ''You want to know the real me? Open that cupboard to your left.''

He did so, revealing a stash of big foil bags of potato

chips with flavors ranging from barbecue to sour cream and onion. "So this is your secret—you're addicted to junk food," he said, grinning at her over his shoulder.

"Only chips. You can keep the pretzels and the nachos and the sweet stuff...except ice cream, of course. But I warn you—never come between me and a bag of ketchup chips. Not if you value living."

"I'll remember that," Cal said, and pulled out a bag of sour cream and onion, taking it into the living room and sitting down on the chesterfield. He tore open the bag, passed it to Marnie, then took a handful of chips himself, crunching them between his teeth. "Well," he said evenly, washing them down with beer, "I guess I'd better come clean."

Marnie had perched herself on the chesterfield, as well. So she'd be near the chips; nothing to do with Cal. She had no idea what was coming next. On an emotional level, she'd lived her life very predictably the past few years, she realized. The insight hit her with a sudden jolt.

Cal wasn't predictable. Not at all.

He was gazing at the bubbles rising from his beer as though searching for inspiration. He said, not raising his eyes, "It was unfair and cruel of me to suggest that you in any way arranged that meeting between you and Kit at the school. When I found out about the shuffle in the league from Kit's note, I drove right to Faulkner. Seeing you and her together zapped my common sense as well as my brains." He looked up. "I'm sorry, Marnie. I should never have said it was a setup."

She nodded slowly; the shock of coming face-to-face with Kit had knocked her sideways, too. "You're forgiven."

His smile was wry. "The more I see of you, the more I realize you're not capable of being devious. Up front— that's the way you operate."

She said levelly, "Why didn't you tell me Kit had been

asking about me—about her biological mother—for the past few months?''

"Oh, that's easy—I was afraid to.''

"Afraid?''

"Of you,'' he said, again staring down at his beer. "Of what happens to me when I come anywhere near you. Losing Jennifer was terrible and it's not in my plans to get emotionally involved with anyone. Especially not with Kit's birth mother.''

So despite all his talk of making love, he was really only talking about sex; his love belonged to Jennifer. Wondering why this should hurt so much, Marnie took a big mouthful of chips. "Keep going.''

"Kit's been impossible the past week and a half. She was furious with me for not telling her about you right away and she hates your guts because you put her up for adoption. When I tried to tell her otherwise, she wouldn't listen. She bombed her exams last week and all the teachers are complaining about her attitude. I want you to come to the house this weekend and see if we can talk any sense into her.''

"Me? To your house?'' As Marnie choked on a chip, Cal whacked her between the shoulder blades. Tears coursing down her cheeks, she gasped, "Okay, okay, that's enough. Cal, she doesn't want to see me. I'd only make it worse.''

"She needs you. Although she'd be the last one to admit it. I don't know what else to do, Marnie!''

"Does she know you're here now?''

"No. She's got basketball practice until six-thirty. I'll have to head back soon.'' In a voice so low she could scarcely hear him, he said, "Please come. Maybe together we can get through to her.''

We... Such a small word to have such huge implications. Feeling her way, Marnie said, "There's no going back, is there? To the way things were three weeks ago. Neither you nor Kit can pretend I don't exist. It's too late for that.''

"I love her and I hate seeing her so unhappy. I feel so helpless to fix it—that's even worse.''

He'd been helpless to prevent Jennifer's death, too, Marnie thought. "I'll come," she said, and regretted the words as soon as they left her mouth. If she'd lived the past thirteen years guarding herself from hurt, to go to Cal's house to confront her daughter's hostility was the worst of moves.

Yet if she was to succeed in breaking through Kit's hostility, the rewards would be wonderful. Feeling her hunger for a true relationship with her daughter like an ache in her throat, Marnie dug into the bag for more chips.

''You'll come?'' Cal said.

She swallowed a mouthful of chips that tasted like sawdust. "That's what I said. Didn't you think I would?''

"I wasn't laying any bets." He took her hands in his and chafed them. "Don't look so frightened. It'll all work out.''

His fingers were lean and strong and very warm, the back of his hands dusted with dark hair. In fascination, she watched the tendons move under his skin. She blurted, "You know so much about her—everything I've missed all those years she was growing up. Yes, I'm frightened. I'm afraid I'll get hurt even worse than I was before.''

He pulled her to him, holding her close to his chest; through his shirt she felt the steady pounding of his heart. She had experienced passion in his embrace only a short while ago. To feel such utter security was almost as novel as the passion, and just as disturbing. She'd always been independent; Charlotte Carstairs had seen to that. What if she grew to need Cal? That could be every bit as dangerous as seeing Kit again. Then she heard him murmur against her hair, ''You're even more courageous than I thought.''

With every nerve in her body, Marnie was aware of the

slide of his lips from her hair to her mouth. If she kissed him back, she'd be lost, she thought, and opened to him with a generosity she hadn't suspected was hers to share; perhaps it had gone underground years ago. "Mmm," she murmured, "sour cream and onion, my favorite flavor of kiss," and felt laughter tremble in his chest. Then he was pushing her down on the chesterfield, his weight and warmth making her head swim. She buried her hands in his hair, kissing him back with an ardor as vibrant as it was inexperienced, and felt him stroke her breast to its peak, his fingers molding her flesh through her shirt until she arched against him in a rage of hunger.

Cal shoved the shirt away from her body to touch the silken expanse of her belly. Rearing up on one elbow, he watched her face as he moved again to her breast, pushing aside her bra to roam her naked skin. Marnie's eyes widened, her lips parting; nothing remotely as powerful as this had brought her and Terry together.

She'd been waiting for Cal. Waiting for years to experience the fierce attraction possible between male and female, to comprehend why her body had been fashioned the way it was. "Oh, Cal," she whispered. "Cal…"

CHAPTER EIGHT

THROUGH the open windows, the soft wash of waves on the shore was suddenly routed by the crunch of tires in the driveway. Marnie sat bolt upright, pushing Cal away, her eyes wide with horror.

"Christine," she sputtered. "She said she was going to bring me some eggs from the farm up the road; I forgot all about it. She mustn't find us like this. She'll be convinced we've been making love all over the floor. I might just as well put a sign up on the road—Marnie Has A Man."

Her cheeks were flushed, and under her dismay some of the dazzlement of Cal's lovemaking still lingered in her face. "Good idea," Cal said. "The sign, I mean. It'll keep the rest of them away."

"There isn't any rest, I keep telling you that," Marnie said irritably. "Stop looking so pleased with yourself, Cal. I—"

A knock came on the door. "Are you in, Marnie?" Christine called.

Marnie tumbled off the chesterfield, smoothed down her shirt and walked across to open the door. "Hello, Chris," she said.

"I saw a Jeep parked by the road. Have you got company?" Christine asked. She was holding two plastic bags in her hand. Then she saw Cal standing by the chesterfield and gave him an ingenuous smile. "Oh, hello."

In a resigned voice, Marnie said, "Chris, meet Cal Huntingdon, a—a friend of mine. Cal, Christine Turner, my best friend. She teaches at the same school as me."

"I'm very pleased to meet you," Christine said.

To her chagrin, Marnie noticed that the cushions on the

chesterfield were crushed where Cal had been lying on top of her. Chris wouldn't miss that charming little detail. She said quickly, "Want a coffee?"

"I can't stop. Don's waiting for me. Here are the eggs and a couple of trout he caught last night. You could cook them for supper for Cal."

"He's not staying," Marnie said repressively. "Are the trout cleaned?"

"Now, Marnie...you've never forgiven Don for bringing you that bass last summer, have you?"

"It was as ugly as sin and all its guts were hanging out."

Cal laughed. His teeth were very white in his tanned face; the crescent-shaped scar over his eye was also white. If she followed her instincts rather than her brains, Marnie knew she'd be pushing him back on the cushions and kissing him senseless.

Perhaps her thoughts showed. Cal's smile deepened, his gaze lingering on her mouth. "Well," Christine said with a seraphic smile, "I'd better go." She proffered the bag, which had been dripping on the floor ever since she arrived. "Maybe you could put these in the freezer and Cal can come back another time."

"Good idea," Cal said promptly.

Glowering at both of them, Marnie said, "When you two have finished arranging my life—"

"Not your life, Marnie," Cal said piously. "I wouldn't think of trying to arrange your life. Just one meal. I like them panfried, by the way, with homemade pickles and lemon meringue pie to follow."

Christine smiled. "Marnie took one of her lemon pies to the Ladies' Aid auction and every guy in the place was bidding on it."

"Chris, you shouldn't keep Don waiting any longer," Marnie said pointedly.

"Nice meeting you, Christine," Cal said. "I'm sure I'll see you again."

"I hope so," Christine replied with undoubted sincerity. "Bye, Marnie. Have a great evening."

The screen door slapped shut behind her. Marnie said roundly, "Those damned trout are dripping all over my clean floor and now Christine's convinced I've finally caught myself a man."

"When's the next Ladies' Aid auction?" Cal asked. "Although I reckon I'd have to sell some shares to be able to afford one of your pies."

"You, buying my lemon pie? In full view of the Ladies' Aid? Now that would really ruin my reputation."

Cal's eyes were twinkling. "I can't think of anything I'd rather do than ruin your immaculate reputation," he said. "You know what? I have fun with you, Marnie."

She tilted her head. "You're referring to Chris's visit, I presume? Not to what she interrupted on the chesterfield."

"Both."

"I'd have been mortally insulted if you'd replied otherwise," Marnie said saucily, and wondered how long it had been since she'd flirted with a man. A very long time. Too long. Because flirting with Cal was fun, too.

Cal looked at his watch. "Hell, I've got to go. Kit'll be home by quarter to seven and I want to be there."

Marnie, for the space of half an hour, hadn't even thought about Kit. A man's slate blue eyes and long-limbed body had made her forget her own daughter. Suddenly frightened, she heard Cal add, "Why don't you arrive mid-morning on Saturday, Marnie? I'll tell her you're coming."

"Maybe she'll leave town," Marnie said, not altogether facetiously.

"She won't. I'll see to that."

Marnie bit her lip. "Around eleven?"

"Plan to stay for lunch—and don't look so scared. I'm beginning to realize it's been inevitable that you'll spend time with Kit ever since I bumped into you in the parking lot."

"Even though both of you have been fighting it all the way?"

"You think I'm not afraid of being hurt again? After Jennifer?" Cal said with sudden violence, and ran his fingers through his hair in a gesture she already knew meant he was upset. "Of course I am."

Marnie wasn't going to ask if Cal still loved his wife; she was ninety percent sure she already knew the answer. She said edgily, "I'll see you Saturday, then."

Cal took the trout and eggs from her, marched them into the kitchen and deposited them on the counter. She heard the tap run as he washed his hands, then he came back into the living room and took her in his arms very naturally, as if saying goodbye to each other was something they'd done often. "Thanks for agreeing to see Kit," he said, and kissed her.

For Marnie, any notion of fun had collapsed as soon as Cal had mentioned the meeting with Kit again. She stood stock-still in his embrace, aware of holding back, wanting him gone so she could be alone to think about all that had happened since his appearance on the beach.

Cal raised his head and said tersely, "I'll tell you one thing. I won't rest until I get you in my bed. Take care, Marnie."

Again the screen door banged shut. A few moments later, she heard the Cherokee drive away. Marnie sat down hard on the rocker, noticing he'd left his tie behind.

She'd been a fool to agree to go back to Burnham.

Kit, her daughter, hated her; nor was Marnie as hopeful as Cal that one visit would change that. And then there was Jennifer, whose house she was going to enter, whose husband wanted Marnie in his bed yet was afraid of getting hurt again.

With every meeting between herself and Cal, she was getting more deeply embroiled. Yet events had gone too far for her to extricate herself.

Marnie went into the kitchen, wrapped the trout in foil and put them in the freezer. Then she mopped up the floor by the front door.

On Saturday morning at four minutes past eleven, Marnie turned down the curving driveway to the cedar-shingled bungalow on Moseley Street. She was wearing cream-colored trousers and a matching crocheted sweater; her hair shone, and she'd put on more makeup than usual to shore up her confidence. Her heart was jouncing against her ribs like a jackhammer.

She had absolutely no idea what she was going to say to Kit. Anything she'd tried to rehearse had sounded fabricated, condescending or sentimental.

She'd wing it. She'd have to.

That she also had to face Cal this morning she was choosing to ignore. Cal, who a couple of days ago had driven a hundred miles to apologize to her and to ask for her help. One thing at a time, she thought, and got out of the car.

The fog had rolled back out to sea only an hour ago; little drops of water clung to the pine boughs, sparkling in the sun, and the grass was wet with dew. Early tulips, pink and white, mingled with the dwarf junipers that flanked the stone walk to the front door. Had Jennifer planted them?

Then the door opened and Cal stepped out into the sunshine. "I thought I heard your car," he said easily. "How are you, Marnie?"

He made no move to kiss her or even take her by the hand. Of course not, thought Marnie. Because she was on his turf now. His and Kit's. And wasn't that the heart of the dilemma? Kit didn't want her at all. Whereas Cal wanted her only on his terms: a secretive affair, nothing in the open. She said succinctly, "I'm scared. How about you?"

"Kit just got up. She's making pancakes. Why don't we go inside and join her?"

"I asked how you were, Cal."

"I like that sweater. It has holes in interesting places."

Trying hard not to blush, Marnie said, "How are you isn't a very complicated question."

"I'm fine," he said blandly. "I like the color of your lipstick, too."

"It's called Juicy Tangerine."

"It clashes with the tulips."

The words were out before Marnie could stop them. "Did Jennifer like to garden?"

"She did," he said expressionlessly. "Come on in, I'll show you around the downstairs before we join Kit."

His whole face had closed against her. Marnie stalked past him into the sunlit entrance hall, which led into a living room centered around a fireplace built out of rough-edged beach stones and flanked by bookshelves. The carpet was Oriental, the furnishings an eclectic mix of antique and modern, and the few paintings ranged from landscapes to abstracts. The room looked lived-in, comfortable and welcoming.

To Marnie, it was infused with the past, with the spirit of a woman who had died too young. In a poignant moment of truth, she sensed she would have liked Jennifer. And perhaps Jennifer would have liked her.

She couldn't share this with Cal.

Cal was discussing the collection of miniature ivory sculptures on the mantel, behaving as though she was a stranger. She could have been a real-estate agent, or someone who'd dropped in for coffee, Marnie thought with an inappropriate spurt of anger.

He didn't look nervous. He didn't look upset. He didn't even look human, for heaven's sake.

And she couldn't do one thing about it. Not here. Not now.

"What a lovely room," she said, and followed him into a dining room whose cherry wood furniture was far from new, yet very beautiful. Absently, her fingers rubbed a nick in the edge of the oval table, on which stood a tall vase of daffodils.

"Kit did that," Cal said. "Bashed it with her garden trowel."

Marnie's fingers sprang away. History, she thought, Kit's history. This house holds everything I've missed. Then her gaze fell on an array of family photos on the sideboard. She flinched away from them. "Where is Kit?" she asked, and was proud that she sounded so nearly normal.

For a moment, she thought Cal was going to comment on her reaction. Then he said formally, "This way. Watch the steps. Our cleaning lady likes to wax the floors until they're slippery enough to skate on."

The stairs led past a sunroom that overlooked the water and was charmingly furnished in bamboo and lavish with plants. Marnie would have liked to sit there with a good book and a cup of coffee, soaking up the sunshine that filtered through the pines. On impulse, she walked into it, admiring the lush fronds of a fern that hung from the roof beam, and the pink waxy petals of a cluster of begonias. Again she was aware of Jennifer's presence, a presence as welcoming as the house.

She turned to face Cal, wanting very much to share this with him. But there was something in his stance that made the words die on her lips. She was instantly certain that for him her presence in Jennifer's house was an intrusion, a reawakening of grief. Marnie's presence only served to emphasize Jennifer's absence. Simple. And hurtful in a way that horrified her.

With every ounce of control she possessed, she said, "Another beautiful room."

"Let's go find Kit."

That's why you've come here. Not to invade my personal space. That's what he meant.

Fine, thought Marnie, and walked past him down a hall-way into the kitchen. So when she came face-to-face with her daughter, her head was held high and her eyes were brilliant as the sunlit sea.

The kitchen was at the front of the house. Kit was perched on a stool at the counter, a teen magazine propped up in front of her as she poked at a pile of pancakes swimming in a pool of melted butter and syrup. Marnie's breath caught in her throat. With an inward prayer for wisdom, she said, "Hello, Kit."

Kit ignored her almost to the point of rudeness, then mumbled, "H'lo."

Cal said, "Coffee, Marnie?"

"Thanks." There was a photo on the magazine cover of the latest male heartthrob. Marnie spent five days a week with teenage girls; she began to talk about the blue-eyed icon in the photo, trying to give Kit time to get used to her presence.

Then she asked Kit's opinion of his latest movie. "It wasn't bad," Kit said, then took another mouthful of pancake.

Cal put a mug of coffee in front of her. Marnie poured in cream and added sugar. "Were you and your friends able to get tickets for Céline Dion?" she asked. "I heard kids were lined up outside Metro Centre for three days."

"Six of us are going," Kit said, and stirred her syrup with the tines of her fork.

Kit had yet to look Marnie in the eye. Marnie labored on. Cal, who seemed to have decided that this was between herself and Kit, had picked up the Saturday paper and was making a pretense of reading it. A normal family in their kitchen on a spring weekend, Marnie thought crazily. Whom are we kidding? There's nothing remotely normal about this. And I'd feel a whole lot better if Cal would get lost. She said, "I'd like to see your room, Kit. Would you show it to me?"

Kit had just finished the last bite of pancake. "It's a mess."

"That doesn't matter."

"Okay," the girl said grudgingly, and pushed back the stool so it scraped on the pine floor.

Not looking back to see if Marnie was with her, Kit went out of the kitchen and down a passage that led into another wing of the house. Marnie followed, her thoughts in such a jumble she didn't notice that Cal, soft-footed, was behind her. Was she pushing Kit too hard? Not hard enough? Should she never have come here, despite Cal's urging?

She rather prided herself on her skill in handling adolescents. Today would certainly keep her humble, she decided, and in a single quick glance saw through a partly opened door a bedroom that must be Cal's—the room he would have shared with Jennifer. Wide bed, view of the cove, the softest of pale rose carpets.

She wasn't here today because of Cal. She was here to try to get through to Kit, to build some kind of relationship with her daughter.

So why should the sight of Cal's bedroom bother her so much?

CHAPTER NINE

KIT'S bedroom, although large and sunny, was indeed a mess. A collection of teddy bears was plumped on every available space; posters of rock groups and movie stars were pinned on the walls. The desk was layered with papers, scribblers and books. Marnie looked down at the cover of the book on top of one of the piles. She said, her voice quivering a little in spite of herself, "I read that book when I was the same age as you."

"We have to read it. For school. I hate it," said Kit.

She had stationed herself against the bookshelves. Back to the wall, thought Marnie, and said in deliberate challenge, "You use that word rather a lot. Hate, I mean." Kit shrugged. Stubbornly, Marnie persisted, "I'm just trying to get to know you a little, Kit, that's all, but I guess I shouldn't have asked to see your room."

"I don't care," Kit said.

"I don't think that's true. I think you do care."

"Think what you like."

Marnie said quietly, "You're behaving atrociously, you know that, don't you?"

A flicker of what could have been shame passed through Kit's deep brown eyes, which were so like Terry's. Then it was gone, leaving Marnie to wonder if she'd imagined it. She walked over to the shelves with their small array of framed color photographs, her hands clenched into fists as she forced herself to look at them one by one. Kit as a baby in Cal's arms, a younger and happier Cal, his wife leaning against him. Jennifer. Pretty, as dark-haired as Cal, her

97

smile very sweet. Kit starting school in a little blue dress, her face solemn. Kit and Cal in a canoe, waving their paddles at whoever was taking the picture. Jennifer and Kit at a picnic table, giggling together with an intimacy that hurt Marnie deep inside.

Looking at the last two more closely, Marnie said, "Those photos were taken at Sandy Lake Park, weren't they?"

Kit said, "We always go there the long weekend in May."

"So do I, with my friend Christine," Marnie said, then wondered if it would have been better or worse to have bumped into Kit three years ago, when Jennifer was alive. "I've missed so much of your growing up—there's so much I can never know."

Kit pounced. "That was your choice, wasn't it?"

"It wasn't my choice, no," Marnie said in open contradiction.

Then she gave a nervous start as Cal spoke from the doorway. "Why don't you tell Kit what happened, Marnie? About your mother."

So he'd been standing there the whole time. Spying on her. She said, "I don't think Kit wants to hear it. Any more than she wants me in your house."

"I think she needs to hear it," he said.

She was caught between a rock and a hard place, thought Marnie, glancing from his implacable slate eyes to Kit's defiantly tilted chin, so like her own. But what did she have to lose? Nothing, by the look of Kit. And everything to gain if only she could break through to her.

"Cal, I wish you'd get lost," she said fretfully. "I'm nervous enough as it is, without you listening to every word."

"I'm staying. This is about the three of us."

"There isn't any three of us," Kit cried. "I don't want her here, Dad!"

Her. Perhaps that was the unkindest cut of all, Marnie thought, to be nameless. As though she didn't exist. She said flatly, "My name's Marnie. I do realize Ms. Carstairs doesn't cut it and Mother's definitely out."

"And watch your manners, Kit," Cal said sharply.

"Sorry," Kit mumbled, and kicked at the carpet with the toe of her sneaker. She looked very unhappy.

Marnie had known ever since the confrontation with Cal in the parking lot that in the past thirteen years she'd never stopped loving her daughter. She now was faced with a recalcitrant adolescent rather than an innocent and adorable baby, but that didn't matter two hoots. She loved Kit. As naturally as the leaves on the trees and as unstoppably as the tides. How could it have been otherwise?

That was why she was here. And that was why she'd once again tell her story, this time to Kit, the one the story most concerned.

She did her best. Terry, Charlotte Carstairs, sixteen-year-old Marnie, she described them all, striving to bring them to life in some way that would engage Kit's sympathies. But her voice sounded wooden, and even to her own ears, her story was just that: a story, fabricated and unconvincing. She saw thinly veiled scorn on Kit's face and knew in pure panic that she was failing at something that was desperately important to her.

Twisting the hem of her sweater, she finished awkwardly, "I hardly ever talk about all this, so I'm not used to—all I'm trying to do is show you that I didn't abandon you, Kit. I couldn't try to trace you or get you back. Dave would've been fired from the only kind of job he knew and he had four sons and a wife to support. And Terry would've been beaten up. I couldn't risk that—don't you see?"

"Dad and Mum brought me up to take responsibility for my actions," Kit said with adult precision, for the first time looking Marnie in the eye. "Not to make excuses and tell lies."

"You think that whole story was a lie?"

"You gave me up! I bet you feel real guilty about that. So you've got to square it somehow."

"You and your father certainly think alike," Marnie said tightly. "That was his first reaction, too."

"I wish you'd go back to Faulkner Beach and stay there! Dad and I are doing fine on our own. We don't need you. We never did and we don't now."

"If you didn't need me, Kit, you'd be indifferent to me," Marnie said strongly. "The one thing you're not is indifferent. And if you think I'm going to lie down on the floor like a—a hooked rug for you to wipe your feet on, you don't know me very well. I'm darned if you're going to walk all over me! You were taken from me without my knowledge or consent, and it broke my heart—so much so that I haven't as much as looked at a man since then."

Kit tossed her red curls, so like Marnie's, although when she spoke there was an edge of uncertainty in her voice. "Don't tell me you're not after Dad. Every woman for ten miles around thinks I need a new mother and he needs a new wife."

"This is about the two of us. Leave your dad out of it. And I know exactly what we're going to do. Next weekend, we're going to Conway Mills, you and I, and I'll show you the town where it all happened, and you can talk to people who knew my mother, knew what she was like. Maybe then you'll believe me."

"I've got a basketball tournament on Friday and Saturday."

"Then we'll go on Sunday!"

"I'll go, too," Cal said in the kind of voice that brooked no argument. "Kit's my daughter, Marnie. She's not going to meet her grandparents—because that would have to happen, wouldn't it?—without my being there."

Dave and Marylou...how could Marnie have forgotten them?

Because she'd let her emotions get out of hand, that's how.

"We can't go," Marnie said, defeat thinning her voice. "They were so good to me, so kind. I can't turn up on their doorstep after all these years with a granddaughter who hates me."

"Why don't you drive there tomorrow and tell Dave and Marylou, and then we'll all go next Sunday?" Cal suggested. "That way, they'd be prepared."

"That way, you can get your stories together," Kit jeered.

Marnie glared at her daughter. "That's enough! Dave and Marylou are as honest as the day is long and far too smart for me to pull the wool over their eyes. Where's the telephone? I'll see if they're home tomorrow."

Unexpectedly, Cal started to laugh. "If only you two could see yourselves," he said. "You're as alike as two peas in a pod."

"Oh, shut up," Marnie snapped.

"I'm not like her," Kit cried.

Cal crossed the room, put an arm around each of them and pulled them unceremoniously over to Kit's mirror. Faithfully, it reflected two sets of tangled red curls, tip-tilted noses and defiant chins. Smiling unwillingly, Marnie said, "I guess you're right. Although your eyes are just like Terry's, Kit."

For a moment, open curiosity shone in Kit's brown eyes.

Then it vanished. "Australia's halfway around the world," she muttered. "No way he's getting involved with me."

"It's as near as a jet flight," Cal said. "But how about one thing at a time—Conway Mills before Australia. Let's go into the kitchen and you can phone from there, Marnie."

His arm was still snug around Marnie's waist. Although her timing was atrocious, she found herself wondering what it would be like to lean on him the way Jennifer had leaned on him in the photo in the living room, to take strength from him and give to him her own strengths. Comfort him and be comforted.

Love him and be loved?

A risk she'd never taken. A risk she'd be a fool to take with Cal, so wedded to his memories of his sweet-faced wife, so protective of his red-haired daughter.

She pulled free of him. "I'll have to call information for their number."

A couple of minutes later, she was standing in the kitchen listening to the phone ring in a house in Conway Mills, the house that had given her love and companionship while she was growing up. Someone picked up the receiver and a man's voice said, "Hello?"

Marnie paled, her free hand gripping the edge of the counter. "*Terry*?"

"Yeah...this is Terry."

"It can't be you—you're in Australia."

"Marnie! Great timing. I was going to call you later today and see if we could get together. How are you?"

"Okay," she said. "How long have you been home?"

"Just got in yesterday. Flying to Montreal for meetings all next week, then back on the weekend. After that, Vancouver and Hong Kong."

Terry's energy had always outstripped Marnie's; he

wasn't one to sit and contemplate the roses. She said, "You haven't changed."

"It's been five years, Mar," he said, using her old nickname. "Can we get together? I should've written after your mum died, but you know me and letters."

Marnie bit her lip, her mouth suddenly dry. "That's why I was phoning, to see if I could come up tomorrow. Or maybe even today. Terry, something's happened...the baby, the one we had...she's here. In the room with me. I—"

"Spill the beans," Terry said.

Using just those same words he had elicited from her all her joys and woes when she was five and ten and fifteen. Frantically, her gaze flew around the sunlit kitchen. Kit was glued to the floor, her mouth hanging open. Cal was standing like a statue in a patch of shadow, tense as a predator. Picking her words, Marnie gave Terry an edited version of the past three weeks.

"Kit's upset," she said. "It's not that long since her mother died. So we thought it might help if we all came together to see your parents. But I was going to come this weekend to tell them about Kit. I can't just arrive with her and her father. I wasn't expecting you to be home."

"They know," Terry said.

Again Marnie felt the floor heave under her. "They *know*?"

"I told them—"

"We agreed you wouldn't!"

"Stop interrupting. To be accurate, Mum sat me down one time and asked me if you'd had a baby all those years ago. It was on my first visit home after you'd told me, actually."

"She asked?" She sounded like an echo, Marnie thought

faintly; her wits seemed to have flown clean out the window.

"Marnie, my parents aren't dumb. They knew you and I were a number. They knew you disappeared and never came back. Mum was talking about how many of her friends had grandchildren, and then right out of the blue she popped the question about the baby. You know me, I never could lie to her."

"Why didn't they mention it when I saw them last month?"

"They were waiting for you to bring it up."

"Oh, God," Marnie said.

"I'll tell 'em you're coming. If it's any comfort, they gave me hell. About the baby, I mean."

It was no comfort at all. "If they already know about Kit, I won't come until next weekend. I hate going back to Conway."

"That figures." Then Terry's voice changed. "If you come next weekend, I'll get to meet her, too. Kit, I mean."

Marnie hadn't even thought of that. Her head whirling, she muttered, "Terry, I can't handle this...I'll call you back in a few minutes." She crashed the receiver down and stared blindly at the dark green ceramic tile on the counter; she was breathing as fast as though she'd been running.

Then Cal was beside her, taking her by the shoulders. He said roughly, "What's wrong, Marnie? Tell me what's wrong."

Her body shuddered in his grasp. And then she did what she'd been longing to do ever since she'd arrived here; she leaned her whole weight on him and closed her eyes. "Hold on to me," she whispered. "Just for a minute."

Through the tangle of emotion that was racketing through her frame, Marnie was achingly aware of his warmth and solidity, of the clean male smell of his skin through his shirt, of his quickened heartbeat. For the first time in her life, she sensed that she'd truly come home. That this was where she belonged. Right here in Cal's arms.

If only she could stay here forever.

She had to call Terry back.

A plate scraped on the counter. She looked up. The hostility on Kit's face could have cracked any number of plates; Marnie pushed herself free of Cal. "S-sorry," she faltered, not looking at him, "that's not like me—"

"Don't apologize," Cal said harshly. "You've carried too much on your own for too long."

"Terry's home," she said in a voice she hardly recognized as her own. "And Dave and Marylou have known I had a baby for the past five years." She sank onto the nearest stool and put her head in her hands. "They'd guessed, so they asked Terry. I haven't seen him for five years, so I didn't know."

"How long is he home?" Cal asked.

It was, of course, a crucial point. Marnie looked over at Kit. "He's leaving tomorrow for Montreal. But he'll be back in Conway next weekend before he heads out to Vancouver. You could meet him, Kit."

Kit's hostility had given way to pure panic. Somewhat heartened, for panic made Kit seem more vulnerable, more like the twelve-year-old she was, Marnie added, "But only if you want to."

Kit's gaze flew to Cal. "Dad?" she said uncertainly.

"If we're going to Conway, we might as well go the whole hog," Cal said, his smile not quite reaching his eyes. "Grandparents and a father...it'll be quite the weekend."

Kit blurted, "What does he look like?"

Marnie said, "He's tall, almost as tall as your dad—he was our high school's champion basketball player. He's nice-looking, with brown hair and eyes just like yours. His mind is like a steel trap when it comes to numbers and he's got tons of energy. He's a good man, Kit.''

"Are you going to marry him?"

Marnie said evenly, "No. We were the best of friends for years, but I never loved Terry that way."

"You had me, though."

Searching for the right words, Marnie said, "We were young and we'd been at the school dance and a harvest moon was shining on the lake—it can happen like that, Kit. It also ruined the friendship. That's why we were out of touch for years."

Cal made a restive movement. "Why don't you call him back, Marnie? Say we'll arrive Saturday evening—the basketball tournaments usually end around three. There must be a motel where we could stay."

That word "we" again, Marnie thought in a panic every bit as real as Kit's. Whether she wanted it or not, events seemed to be picking her up and carrying her along like a roller coaster. With a strange sense of fatality, she dialed again.

"That you, Marnie?"

"Yes...sorry about that. Could we come late next Saturday?"

"Sure. I spoke to Mum and Dad. You can stay here, there's lots of room."

"Cal had thought a motel—"

"Since the new highway went in, the motel went out of business."

So that was that. "Okay," Marnie said. "We'll see you then. Say hello to your mum and dad for me."

"Will do. Stay out of trouble."

It was a phrase from their shared childhood. She said with asperity, "That's just what we didn't do."

He was laughing as she put down the receiver. She said

rapidly, "Cal, the motel's closed. We can stay with Dave and Marylou."

"Well, that's certainly plunging in the deep end," he said, his features inscrutable. "Kit, I don't know how you'll concentrate on your game next weekend. And now, how about if we rustle up something for lunch?"

Marnie said with a touch of desperation, "I can't stay. I feel as though I've been run over by a truck. I need to go home and walk the beach for a while."

"There's a perfectly good beach below the house."

"Please, Cal..." Marnie said, and saw a flash of triumph on Kit's face. Kit was glad she was leaving. Exhaustion washed over Marnie like a tidal wave. She said thinly, "Goodbye, Kit, I'll see you next weekend. Good luck with your games."

Kit gave her an inimical look. Cal said, "I'll see you out."

Marnie would have much preferred he didn't. She headed for the front door and hurried past the tulips, which had opened their pink and white cups to the sun. But as she reached for the car door, Cal stopped her, his hand on her arm.

"Don't be in such an all-fired hurry."

"I need to be alone!"

"I know Kit's behaving badly. But my gut tells me that meeting her father and grandparents will be good for her."

Marnie said forcefully, "Terry is her father in name only—you're her real father."

His face was shuttered. "She wants to meet him."

"I spent an hour on the lakeshore with Terry. You've spent thirteen years with Kit. No contest. You don't have a worry in the world."

"I'm not worrying!"

She managed a small smile. "Yes, you are. You're afraid

of losing her, and guess what, we're arguing again. Maybe I'll go home and paint some vertical stripes."

Cal gave a choke of laughter. "A whole wall full of them. I want you to do me a favor."

"What?" she said warily.

"Are you free Wednesday evening?" She nodded. "Kit's staying with Lizzie that night...the teachers have a training session the next morning. Let's go to Halifax. Have dinner, see a movie, talk about anything and everything under the sun except my daughter, your best friend Terry and Conway Mills."

"A date," Marnie said uneasily.

"You catch on fast."

"Cal, Kit can't stand the sight of me, you hated my being in your house, and I'm scared of men. And you're talking about a *date*? Give me a break."

"What's the alternative? Play it safe? Put your canoe in at the top of the rapids and then head for shore? Maybe that'd work for other people, Marnie. But not for you and me."

Was he right? Certainly the thought of spending a whole evening with Cal filled her with the same excitement she felt stemming a chimney in a granite cliff. "Then we're crazy."

"Probably." He rubbed the back of his neck. "Look at it another way. You and I will be seeing a lot of each other from now on because of Kit. So we might as well get to know one another."

"You're rationalizing!"

"I'm trying to get through to you," he grated.

"I have to build my own relationship with Kit—one that's got nothing to do with you."

"Get real, Marnie," Cal muttered. Then, moving too fast for her to evade him, he stepped closer and kissed her, a fierce, demanding kiss that set her blood surging through her veins as rampantly as any rapids. "How's that for an argument?" he said.

"So I go off like a firecracker whenever you kiss me," she fumed. "Are you planning on getting me into bed on Wednesday since Kit has a sleepover—step one in your campaign for a fifty-miles-apart affair?"

He looked every bit as furious as her. "When we go to bed together, it won't be because one of us planned it. It'll be because we both want to."

"Count me out, Cal. That's one cliff I have no intention of climbing."

"Let's try another metaphor. You've made celibacy into a very comfortable little cage, and now you're busily throwing away the key."

"It *isn't* a cage! Anyway, you're the one who said you didn't want to get involved again because of Jennifer."

"Then I'm making a liar out of myself." He looked around at the tall trunks of the pines as if he wasn't quite sure where he was, then turned back to Marnie. "I loved my wife," he said unevenly. "But I never once in all the years of our marriage felt as though I'd die if I couldn't make love to her."

Marnie's face was blank with shock. "But—"

"You and I...it's different from what it was with Jennifer, that's what I'm getting at. There's no comparison. So I don't know the rules. Don't know what the devil's going on."

Marnie said with painful intensity, "You're telling the truth, aren't you?"

"Oh, yes."

"I don't understand!"

"You think I do?" He hesitated. "Let me tell you something else, Marnie. I knew the day we met in the thunderstorm that at some deep level I needed you in my life. Sure, I wanted you. Still do. But I'm talking need. Nothing to do with Kit and everything to do with me. It half killed me that afternoon to send you away. That's probably where my jackass suggestion about an affair came from. Please...just give us a chance to get to know each other, that's all I'm asking.''

Shaken by his plea, for he wasn't a man to use words carelessly, Marnie whispered, ''If we go out on a date and you don't have to go home afterward, we'll end up in bed. I know we will. I'm too scared, Cal!''

''I'll make sure we don't—I swear.''

''It doesn't really make any difference, don't you see?'' she said passionately. ''Kit doesn't want me anywhere near you. That's why I have to establish my own relationship with her. And I won't risk being hurt again by a man, I won't.''

''I'd never intentionally hurt you.''

I'm afraid of falling in love with you.... The words echoed in Marnie's brain; she had no idea where they'd come from. ''No, Cal,'' she whispered, ''I can't.''

She was right, she knew she was. Every nerve in her body was screaming at her to run from Cal as fast as she could. Cage or no cage, she was right. But somehow she had to end this before she started blubbering like a baby.

''I'll see you Saturday,'' she said. ''Call me when you're ready to leave.''

''You're doing yourself a disservice as much as me,'' he said tightly.

''I don't agree.'' He was standing very still, his face masked by shadows. He was, she thought unhappily, far too civilized a man to force her and much too proud to plead again. ''Goodbye,'' she mumbled, and got into her car. To her infinite relief, it started like a charm and drew away from the bungalow in fine style.

She didn't pull over on Moseley Street to cry her eyes out and she didn't cry when she got home. Why cry, when she'd done what she knew was right? But her house, which usually welcomed her, did indeed feel like a cage.

She phoned a couple of her buddies and went canoeing on the LaHave River, ending with a barbecue at dark. On Sunday, she and Mario scaled the north buttress at Paces Lake. Marnie loved climbing because it required the utmost in concentration, agility and nerve. She kept her focus on the buttress because she was first leader; but when they did some bouldering on the way home, she slipped twice, grazing her knee and her elbow.

She couldn't tell Mario what was the matter. She couldn't tell anyone. Christine, she knew, would urge her to go on the date with Cal. So she wasn't going to tell Christine how unhappy she felt; how the image of Cal's shadowed face had intruded itself between her and the rock face and caused her to lose her balance, her foot skidding from its toehold.

She played with Midnight on the beach on Sunday evening, then jogged for half an hour, ignoring the pain of her scraped knee so she'd be tired enough to sleep. On Monday after school, she went on a ten-kilometer hike with a couple of the teachers, then invited them in for a late supper, drank too much wine and spent most of Tuesday feeling absolutely rotten.

As Marnie walked home from school that afternoon, a thick mist had blurred the horizon, gentling the harsh outline of the rocks along the shore. The waves rose and fell. Out beyond the point, the marker buoy, invisible, clanged on the swell; the foghorn on the lighthouse boomed its repetitious warning.

Warning of danger.

What was she going to do this evening? Run three rapids and climb a couple of mountains? Then jog a marathon? She'd done nothing but run—one way or another—ever since Cal had asked her for a date.

Ever since she'd turned him down.

She went home and fought against the temptation to phone someone—anyone—who'd keep her too busy to face all her fears and her unease. Instead, she cooked supper and ate it alone, gazing through the window as the fog came closer, her circle of vision getting smaller and smaller.

Isn't that what she was doing with her life? Constricting it? Sure, she had wonderful friends and she could scale a 5.9 pitch and go solo down the Penobscot River; she also loved her job and knew without vanity that she did it well.

But none of that was enough. Not since she'd met Cal and Kit.

She could only hope that the visit to Conway Mills would somehow break through Kit's distrust; even the most tentative of friendships with Kit would be enough for Marnie. She loved her daughter. She wanted her in her life.

And then there was Cal, with his deep voice and his powerful body and his admission that he needed her.

She wanted him, too. Wanted to make love with him. Against all her fears, through all the walls she'd built around herself for so long, she longed to be in his arms and face with him what seemed like an insurmountable danger. He'd help her...wouldn't he?

She paced up and down. She took out her paints and produced a canvas where dark and light swirled together, inextricably entangled. She put a defiant blob of yellow paint bright as any sunrise right in the middle of the swirls, then took a shower and got dressed in jeans and a purple mohair sweater with dangly copper earrings and her new leather sandals.

Then Marnie got in her car and drove to Burnham.

114   THE MOTHER OF HIS CHILD

to the windows. As far as she could tell, both bedrooms
were in darkness.

Maybe Cal was asleep, too.

Maybe not, came less reassuring...

Part of her, the sensible part, believed to find him
impossible. But it was the other side of Marnie, the side

CHAPTER TEN

IT WAS half past ten when Marnie turned left onto Moseley
Street. She drove past Cal's bungalow; lights shone in the
kitchen, and the Cherokee was parked in the driveway. She
went a couple of hundred feet farther along the road, did a
U-turn and parked her car, locking it before walking back
along the shoulder of the road to the bungalow.

She had no idea what she was going to do when she got
there.

The light was still on in the kitchen, which was empty.
She could ring the front doorbell. But what if Kit answered?

In sheer terror, Marnie stopped in her tracks. The worst
thing in the world would be for Kit to find Marnie skulking
around the house in the dark.

She shouldn't be here.

But then the image of Cal's face, strained and unhappy,
dropped into Marnie's mind. It hadn't been easy for Cal to
tell her he needed her.

If only she could have both of them. There was room in
her heart for both, surely. Yet right now Cal had to be her
priority, she knew that instinctively. And Kit was almost
certainly asleep; it was a school night after all.

Giving her head a little shake, Marnie padded around the
end of the house, ready at the slightest sign of life to run
for cover. Her feet were cold, and her toenails, which she'd
painted purple to match her sweater, were already wet from
the grass. She stood still under the pines, breathing in their
fragrance as she tried to orient herself by assigning rooms

to the windows. As far as she could tell, both bedrooms were in darkness.

Maybe Cal was asleep, too.

Maybe she'd come here for nothing.

Part of her, she knew, would be relieved to find him unavailable. But it was the other side of Marnie, the side that had made her sign up for a class on rock climbing, that now impelled her out of the shelter of the pines to cross the uneven ground below the house. She skirted several yews and some rhododendrons loaded with fat buds, then froze to stillness.

There was a basement level to the house. From a bank of low windows, light fell across a rock pathway edged with heather that was already in bloom. Through the windows, Marnie could see Cal.

The room was a miniature gymnasium complete with weight machines. Wearing a pair of sweatpants and a T-shirt, Cal was working a horizontal lever that lifted a pile of metal slabs; his back was to her. Even from that distance, she could see that his hair was soaked with sweat.

He let go of the lever, stretching his arms around the back of his neck one by one. As he turned to face her, staring out into the darkness, she shrank back into the shadows. He stripped off his T-shirt, wiping his face with it before tossing it to the floor, then moved to a set of barbells. Crouching, he lifted them to rest on his thighs, then, with an elegance she had to admire, smoothly lifted them to shoulder height. The muscles were corded in his belly.

Dry-mouthed, she watched as he repeated the lifts again and again. He looked like a man driven. As though he couldn't stop even if he wanted to.

Very much like herself the past three days.

Cal increased the weights, his face contorted with effort. Then he dropped the bar to the floor; even from that distance she could see he was panting. He walked over to a window, leaning against the wooden frame and gazing into the mist. Suddenly, he dropped his forehead to the glass and closed his eyes, his shoulders slumped in utter defeat.

Cut to the heart, Marnie didn't even stop to think. A shower of water dripped down her neck as she pushed her way past a rhododendron bush and into the open. She stepped over the heather to the path, her eyes glued to him, willing him to look up.

He didn't. So she walked boldly toward the glass and tapped on it with her knuckles.

Cal's head jerked up. He was looking straight at her, staring at her as though she were a ghost, an apparition called up by the mist from the sea. Or else an enemy, she thought. Her heart thumping uncomfortably hard under her mohair sweater, Marnie held her ground.

Slowly, Cal straightened. He walked past her, and for the first time, she saw a door set in the wall to the right of the windows. He pulled it open, yellow light spilling over the rock path. "You'd better come in," he said.

Definitely an enemy, Marnie decided, and walked past him, her chin held high. She felt as frightened as that day when she'd first taken the leader's position on a climb on Eagles's Nest. Frightened and determined not to show it, and equally determined to do the very best she could to get to the top without any false moves.

She turned to face him. "Is Kit asleep?" As he nodded, she said unevenly, "You don't look very pleased to see me."

"Don't I?" Cal said unpleasantly.

"No, you don't! Do you still want to go on a date with me tomorrow?"

"It depends."

He'd recovered his poise. His gaze was watchful, his

stance loose, his sweatpants slung low on his hips. Dark
hair curled between his nipples and funneled to his navel,
and he was still breathing hard from his exertions. She'd
never realized just how impressively his torso was muscled.
Or how totally distracting those muscles could be.

When you were climbing as leader for the very first time,
you couldn't afford the slightest distraction.

"Cal," Marnie said, "it's my turn to eat crow and you're
not making it one bit easy and I do wish you'd put your
T-shirt on."

He raised one brow. "It stinks."

"By the looks of you, I'm not going to get close enough
for that to be an issue."

"Oh, you never want to count on that, Marnie," Cal said
with menacing softness.

Her tongue tripping over the words, she asked, "Have
you missed me since Saturday?"

"Why don't I ask you the same question? After all,
you're the one who said no date."

"Since Saturday afternoon, I've canoed, hiked, run,
climbed and bouldered, and drunk too much wine. Oh, and
painted a picture. Yes, I've missed you."

A gleam of devilment shot through his slate blue irises.
"Vertical stripes?"

"Swirls," she said. "Black-and-white swirls, all mixed
up. The way I feel when I'm anywhere near you."

"So which color won out—black or white?"

"I'm here, aren't I?" Her smile was defiant. "The last
thing I did was put a big blob of yellow smack-dab in the
middle."

"Come here."

With a more convincing smile, she asked, "You
wouldn't be telling me what to do, would you?"

"Please, Marnie, darling Marnie, come here."

Shaken to the tips of her sandals by his endearment, feeling as though she were stepping off the edge of a cliff into thin air, Marnie walked closer. When she was within six inches of him, she stopped, her eyes wide.

He said gravely, "You're very wet," and tweaked one of her curls.

The mist had dewed her hair and her sweater. "My sandals are probably ruined."

He glanced down and gave a sudden laugh. "Purple toenails. I'm flattered."

"I rather thought they might be the finishing touch."

"Oh, I was finished the moment I saw you," he said. "What about your fingernails—purple, too?"

He took her hands in his, spreading them flat. Her nails were innocent of polish, her supple fingers bare of rings, her knuckles grazed. "What happened there?" he asked.

"I was jamming a crack in the granite on Sunday. That's always hard on the hands."

"Don't explain it to me. I don't want to know," Cal said grimly. "I don't think I could bear watching you climb."

"No more than I could bear watching you face a truckload of rebels armed with machine guns."

"That's different."

"Sure it is—a higher danger quotient." She added abruptly, "Cal, am I way out of line to have come here this evening and risked Kit seeing me? *Do* you still want to go on a date with me tomorrow night?"

He raised her hand to his mouth, gently brushing her scraped flesh with his lips, a gesture that touched her to the heart. Then he said formally, "Marnie Carstairs...is Marnie your real name, by the way?"

"Maureen." She grimaced. "That's what my mother always called me. I've been Marnie to everyone else for years."

"Marnie suits you much better. I can't imagine a Maureen hanging by her fingernails from a cliff."

"The only time in my life I've ever done that is right now," she said tersely, glancing down at his naked chest.

His lashes flickered. "Yes, I want to spend tomorrow evening with you, of course I do. And I won't even kiss you, if that's what it takes."

Nor would he. She knew it in her bones. Knew she could trust him. He was like the anchors and ropes that gave protection to a climb even though you didn't use them. The anchors that allowed you to climb free.

And all of a sudden, there was no danger. Marnie rested her hands on his shoulders, reached up and kissed him with a mixture of shyness and certainty that revealed more, perhaps, than she realized. With a smothered groan, Cal strained her to him, deepening the kiss, his tongue searching out the sweetness of her mouth, his hands roaming the soft, damp folds of her sweater, then moving lower to press her hips to his.

The heat of his bare flesh beneath her palms intoxicated Marnie. She let her fingers wander the smooth, sweat-sleek plane of his breastbone, then cup the hard curves of his rib cage, an exploration whose intimacy shifted her to a place she'd never been before. As Cal's lips slid to her throat, she whispered, "Do you know what?"

He looked up, the expression on his face making her tremble. "No," he said, "I don't. Unpredictable's your middle name."

Very deliberately, she pressed her palms to his belly, feeling the muscles contract involuntarily as she did so, teasing his body hair with her fingertips. "I've just discovered something I never understood. What the word 'erotic' really means," she said. Her nails trailed to his navel, her heart thudding as she saw his face constrict at her touch. "I didn't know before. I've never experienced it, you see."

He said very quietly, "You take my breath away."

Tears flooded her eyes. "Do I, Cal? Do I really?"

"Yeah...this is new to me, too, the way I am with you. I've never felt this way before. Not in my whole life." He paused, briefly glancing outward into the darkness and the fog. "I'm only going to say this once, Marnie. But I need to say it. I loved Jennifer, you know that. She was sweet and gentle, and I wanted her to be happy. But every now and then, I had to get out. Go overseas, throw myself into the unpredictable, the risky, the dangerous. Even though I took those risks elsewhere—away from her—she hated it when I traveled. She wanted to keep me safe. To know where I was, what I was doing. She couldn't understand that even though I loved her, too much routine and predictability just plain stifled me."

Marnie kept silent, knowing she was learning something key about Cal, deeply grateful that he was telling her so much.

His voice raw, he went on, "Which isn't to say that I wouldn't have died for her if I could. Seeing her suffer at the end...it was terrible. I know that's part of the reason for Kit's behavior. How do you explain suffering to a ten-year-old?"

Again Marnie felt tears swim under her lids. "Thank you for telling me," she said. "Cal, did you hate me for being here in Jennifer's house on Saturday? Because somehow, and maybe this sounds right out to lunch, it seemed as though she was welcoming me."

"No, of course I didn't hate it, and one of the very last things she told me was not to stay a widower for too long. But you've turned my world upside down, Marnie. I can't even begin to tell you what I felt when you stood in the kitchen, walked past my bedroom door.... Dammit, I'm doing a lousy job explaining all this.''

In a flash of intuition, Marnie said, ''During your marriage, did you hide emotions that might be considered unsafe?''

He ran his fingers through his hair, avoiding her eyes. ''I never told Jennifer what it was like not to father my own child. For her, it was all tied up with her identity as a woman. I'm not sure it occurred to her that I'd have feelings around it, too.''

''Then I've discovered two things since Saturday,'' Marnie announced, knowing her words for the truth. ''I don't want to play it safe. And you can tell me anything you like.''

Cal looked at her sharply. ''I can, can't I? Good, bad and indifferent.''

She gave a rich chuckle. '' 'Indifferent' I have a hard time imagining.''

His grin was so full of energy that this time she laughed out loud. ''Marnie,'' he said, ''will you go on a date with me tomorrow?''

''Cal, I would love to.''

''Well,'' he said ironically, ''that was easy.''

''Wasn't it just? What time will you pick me up?''

''Five-thirty. And I promise to feed you something other than dill chips and cherry ice cream—so don't wear your jeans.''

''Or my shorts?''

''We'd never get away from your place if you did that,'' Cal said.

Then he kissed her again, a very comprehensive kiss that filled Marnie with a wild hunger for more. She pressed her body to his, through her jeans feeling his erection with a passionate excitement and no fear whatsoever. Opening to him, she kissed him back, her breasts crushed to his chest.

It was Cal who pulled away, his breathing harsh. "We can't make love—not here, not now. You deserve better of me than that. When we go to bed, I don't want to rush, I don't want to be worrying about Kit hearing us."

For the past few minutes, Marnie had forgotten all about Kit. Plummeted from desire to despair, she faltered, "But if we make love and Kit still hates me, what'll we do?"

"I don't know," Cal said.

In a low voice, Marnie said, "This tears me apart, this seesawing between Kit and you. I just wish I knew what's the right thing to do. For all three of us."

Cal said roughly, "I think we should cool it for now. Even though in some ways I feel like I've known you forever, we met less than a month ago. No heavy-duty kisses tomorrow evening, and I'll keep my hands off you even if it kills me. Which it might."

She couldn't bear the look on his face. She'd learned tonight that an important part of Cal had been refused expression during his marriage: he could only feed his appetite for risk overseas. And what of his appetite for passion? Had Jennifer, with the best intentions in the world, tamed that, too? Safety and the marriage bed, in Marnie's opinion, wouldn't make the best of companions; she was almost willing to bet that Cal had smothered some of his physical needs for the sake of his wife, as well.

So did she, Marnie, free Cal in some way so he could be truly himself? "Were you ever unfaithful to Jennifer?" she asked impulsively, then grimaced. "Not that it's any of my business. Sorry, I shouldn't have asked."

"No, of course I wasn't. In lots of ways, I'm an old-fashioned kind of guy, Marnie. Certainly I took my marriage vows very seriously."

She believed him instantly and said, "I agree with you that we should take one step at a time, Cal. A date. That's what we're talking about and that's all. So which movie will we see?"

"I'll pick up a paper tomorrow and bring it with me."

She gave him her best smile. "I'd better go. Now that I've got what I wanted."

His hand reached out to caress her, then he snatched it back. "Have you, Marnie?"

"Maybe not quite all," she said ruefully. "It might kill me, too. I want you to know that. And now will you walk me to my car? It's parked up the road."

He said abruptly, "I don't think it's just sex. Not anymore."

She blinked. "And you call me unpredictable?"

"Is that all you think it is?"

He was being as honest as he knew how, Marnie thought with a painful constriction of her heart, and he deserved her honesty back. "No," she said. "If sex was all that's between us, I wouldn't be half so scared."

"I like you, Marnie Carstairs," Cal said gruffly. Then he looked around for his T-shirt and pulled it on with the air of a man not quite sure he knew what he was doing. "Why don't we go out this way?" He took her hand as they walked along the path; pine needles had never smelled so pungent to Marnie, or fog so salt laden and mysterious. All too soon they came to her car. "I hope that wreck will get you home," Cal said, kissed her on the cheek and watched as she climbed in.

"It will. Good night, Cal," she said, and drove away, in her rearview mirror seeing a tall, dark-haired man with one hand raised in salute.

As she went around a corner in the road, he disappeared. From nowhere, a question coursed through Marnie's brain:

Was this what love felt like? This unsettling mixture of excitement and discovery, strongly laced with a desire beyond comprehension?

How would she know? She'd never been in love.

She knew one thing. Well, two, actually. Right now, she didn't need to go rock climbing. And she didn't feel alone.

She felt as though Cal was in the car with her, his presence so strong she could almost touch it. Passionate Cal, with his slate blue eyes and his beautiful body and his awkward bursts of honesty.

Cal, who desired her, and who, once more, was smothering his very real needs. This time, for his daughter's sake.

On the way home, Marnie made a detour into the shopping mall at Rockcliffe, between Faulkner Beach and Halifax. She was almost sure she knew what she was going to do.

It had everything and nothing to do with safety.

CHAPTER ELEVEN

MARNIE woke up on Wednesday morning knowing exactly what she was going to do. She got up right away and spent an hour in the kitchen before going off to work. She took her car instead of walking and at noon shopped for groceries. Promptly at three-thirty, she left school and drove straight back home, spending another hour in the kitchen before going to her bedroom, where she laid a single garment from her closet on the bed. Lastly, Marnie had a shower.

When the doorbell rang, she'd just finished putting the finishing touches to her makeup. She gave herself a quick look in the mirror and hurried to the door.

Cal looked extremely handsome in a lightweight gray suit with a pale blue shirt and a silk tie, his hair brushed into some sort of order. He was clutching a bouquet of tawny orange roses. He said with a crooked smile, "We said no sex. But we didn't say no roses. They reminded me of your red hair, Marnie."

"Auburn," she quipped. "But they're lovely, thank you."

He glanced down at her. "I'm too early...you haven't finished dressing."

Talking a little too fast, because now that Cal was here in the flesh, her plan seemed utterly outrageous, she said, "I took sewing lessons a couple of years ago, just long enough to learn that I'm more at home with pitons than a Singer sewing machine. This is the sole result—pretty hard to foul up something that only has two seams and doesn't have to fit.''

She was wearing a long, loose gown patterned in a jungle print of rich oranges, browns and yellows. The sleeves were loose, the neckline—a little crooked because she'd had difficulty with the bias—baring the graceful curve where her neck met her shoulders. Her gold hoops caught the light; her hair was a soft mass of curls.

Cal cleared his throat, carefully keeping his distance from her. ''It clashes with your purple toenails,'' he said. ''We've got lots of time. Most of the late movies don't start until after nine. I've got a newspaper in the car. I thought you could look at it while we're driving.''

Her mouth dry, Marnie said, ''Did you make a dinner reservation?''

He nodded. ''At Pierrot's, down by the harbor.''

It was time to put her plan into action. Or abandon it altogether and never tell him the difference.

What kind of woman was she? She was darned if she was going to play it safe. ''I just have to make a quick phone call,'' she said, taking the phone book out of her magazine rack and looking up the number for Pierrot's. She dialed and when the receiver was picked up said pleasantly, ''I believe you have a reservation for two people this evening...the name's Huntingdon? I'm really sorry, we won't be able to make it. We'll be in another time, I'm sure. Thank you.'' Then she put the phone down.

Cal was standing very still at one end of the chesterfield. Marnie said rapidly, ''There's a bottle of white wine in the refrigerator. Why don't you open it while I get the chips and dip?'' He said nothing. He looked totally at a loss, like someone who'd been knocked right off balance. ''Please?'' Marnie quavered.

Cal ran his fingers around his collar as though it was too tight. "What's going on, Marnie?"

"The wine, Cal."

She'd noticed before how quickly he could move for so big a man; but tonight he was clumsy, bumping into the arm of the chesterfield as he passed it. She trailed after him into the kitchen, wishing her stomach felt less hollow and her nerves less jumpy. Salad dressing, a loaf of garlic bread and a package of wild rice stood on the counter, along with a wooden bowl of sour-cream-and-onion chips and a small bowl of dip. But Cal was staring at the lemon meringue pie that was sitting on a rack by the stove to cool. The meringue had cooperated beautifully, its peaks browned to perfection. He said in a voice she'd never heard him use before, "You made that for me?"

"Yes." She braced her back against the edge of the counter, wishing she could read his mind. "The trout fillets are marinating, ready for the barbecue. Cal, is it okay, what I've done? You don't mind?"

He looked over at her. She knew her cheeks were flushed with nervousness and her eyes glittering for the same reason; but she couldn't have known how vulnerable the curve of her mouth was. "No," he said in the same unreadable voice, "I don't mind."

"There's something else I need to say," Marnie faltered. "I love Kit, she's my daughter. How could I not love her? But this evening isn't about Kit. It's about you and me."

"You and me," Cal repeated, his face expressionless. Then, as if he craved action, he walked past her to the refrigerator, took out the wine bottle, opened it and poured wine into the two glasses sitting on the counter. None of his movements had their usual economy.

He said in a matter-of-fact tone, almost as though he was talking to a stranger, "This is going to sound very obvious, but I'm going to say it anyway. Once we make love, Marnie, there's no going back—we can't undo it. Are you sure you want to?"

Suddenly afraid that he was speaking more to himself than to her, she whispered, "Yes, I do...but what about you?"

His answer was to pass her one glass and raise his own. "To paddling the rapids."

"To scaling the cliff."

For the first time, Cal smiled. "You need to know something about me—I don't even do ladders."

"I don't do guerrillas, Cal," she said, and drank.

He reached over for her glass, put it back on the counter beside his and took her in his arms. She felt the shock run through him as he discovered she was naked beneath her gown. With an inarticulate groan, he lowered his head and kissed her like a man who'd been starving for longer than he could remember and suddenly sees a feast spread before him. A feast such as he couldn't have imagined.

Marnie had never been kissed like that in her life. Every nerve in her body responded; she strained to him, caressing the silky dark hair at his nape, her tongue dancing with his in a way that filled her with delight and desire.

Abruptly, Cal pulled away from her, his expression making her heart sink. "You couldn't have done anything more calculated to make me happy than what you've done here tonight," he said in a chopped voice. "But we can't make love. I didn't bring any protection—figured that way I'd stay honest."

The color deepened in her cheeks. "I thought you might not. So I went to a drugstore last night, one where nobody knows me. The one that's halfway to Halifax and stays open until midnight."

He threw back his head and laughed. "I wish I could've

been a fly on the wall. Now that's what I call living dangerously.''

She said with great dignity, "There was far too much choice, so I grabbed whichever ones were nearest and got out of there as fast as I could. Give me a 5.11 climb any day of the week.''

"Sure you got the right thing?" he teased.

"Cal, I can read as well as the next woman." Her smile was impish. "To further put your mind to rest, Christine and Donald are at a party thirty miles down the road.''

"So what are we waiting for?" Cal said.

The other thing she'd done in her lunch hour was change the sheets on her bed and put a little bunch of sweet-smelling mayflowers on her bureau. Hurriedly, Marnie took a big gulp of her wine, took him by the hand and led him out of the kitchen into her bedroom.

Not for Marnie ruffled sheers and pretty pastels. Her quilt had been made by an old lady from Faulkner; Marnie had fallen in love with its bright squares of primary colors. The rug by her bed was forest green, the curtains the same shade. On the little bedside table was a scented candle and the array of foil envelopes.

She didn't know why she'd bothered with the candle; despite her drawn curtains, it was daylight. Nowhere to hide, she thought, and in sudden terror wondered what she'd do if she didn't like sex with Cal any more than she'd liked it with Terry.

One thing was certain. She wouldn't have the nerve to take her purchases back to the drugstore.

Cal hauled off his jacket, tie and belt, tossed them over her chair and bent to pull off his shoes and socks. Then he said, "Sweetheart, don't look so frightened. I wouldn't hurt you for the world, surely you know that.''

Sweetheart... Marnie repeated silently to herself, and

knew it for the truth. "I'm not scared, not anymore," she said aloud, and walked trustingly into his arms. "Although I don't have a clue how we go about this."

Smiling, he said, "I think you'll soon realize that one thing leads to another."

His hands were firm along the long curve of her spine as he bent to kiss her, a slow, deep kiss of mutual exploration that set Marnie's pulses pounding in her ears. With enthusiasm, if not expertise, she kissed him back, pressing her body into his, suddenly impatient to experience with Cal all that she'd missed for so long. As though he caught her mood, Cal swung her onto the bed, covering her with his body, kissing her as though he'd never kissed a woman before. As though she was the first one, thought Marnie, and fumbled for the buttons on his shirt.

Between them, awkward with haste, they removed his shirt, which fell to the floor beside the bed. Marnie let her mouth slide to the pulse at the base of his throat, then lower, her fingers tangled in his body hair. "You don't know how I've longed to do this," she murmured. "You taste so good."

Her chestnut hair lay on the white sheet like little tongues of fire. Cal threw one thigh over hers and pushed himself up on his elbow, smoothing the silky fabric of her gown over the sweet swell of her breast, over and over again, watching her face as she trembled with pleasure. He said roughly, "I want to see you naked, Marnie," and tugged at the hem of her gown.

In a flurry of fabric, the gown was discarded. Suddenly shy, Marnie lay still beneath him, watching as his eyes roamed her body from the fullness of her breasts to the slight rise of her belly and the juncture of her thighs, then all the way down her smoothly muscled legs to her purple toenails. He said quietly, ''I knew you'd be beautiful…but not this beautiful.''

That he should call her beautiful filled Marnie with pride. With a touch of mischief, she teased, ''Does one thing really lead to another? Then it's your turn,'' and reached for the catch on the waistband of his trousers. Moments later, he, too, was naked, all his male tautness of muscle and tendon exposed to her. She said, ''Lie back a minute, Cal.''

He obeyed her without question. Half-sitting, she let her hands wander his body with a sensuality she wouldn't have known she possessed: through the dark pelt of hair on his chest, around his rib cage, across the jut of his pelvic bones and, finally, to his arousal. As she reached it, his face contorted. ''Marnie, it's been so long, I can't…''

Swiftly, she lay beside him, lifting his hand to her breast, briefly closing her eyes in wonderment as he circled her nipple, then lowered his mouth to the ivory rise of her flesh. Her whole body was aching with a primitive hunger, a single surge of need for Cal to fill her and empty within her. She opened her thighs to gather him in and heard him say in the same hoarse voice, ''There's no rush. We've got all night.''

She didn't want him controlling his own hunger for her sake; she already knew he was a man who'd repressed his nature for too long. She said with sudden urgency, ''Cal, you don't have to play it safe with me. Ever.''

For a moment, he dropped his forehead to rest on her breasts; she could hear his uneven breathing. She stroked his black hair, whispering, ''Are you all right?'' and thought how odd it was that she, who felt almost virginal, should be reassuring Cal, who'd been married for so long.

When he looked up, his slate blue eyes were open to her in a way that was new. ''You have this capacity to shake my soul,'' he muttered, and drew her hard against the lean length of his frame. "You don't know how often I've craved to hold you like this, Marnie, how I've dreamed of you naked and open and willing."

So was this love? she wondered. A man exposing himself body and soul to a woman who only wanted him to be himself? Because the true Cal, the real Cal, was the man who was her mate?

She didn't know the answers to her questions. "I'm so happy to be here with you," she said, her eyes shining like open pools where the currents were deep and sure of themselves. Then Cal spread her hair on the pillow, his face intent, and lowered his head to kiss her again, all the while moving his body over hers until she writhed with need. As he took her breast in his mouth again, she arched against him, frantic for fulfillment. "Please," she said jaggedly, "please, Cal..."

Only then did he touch her where her soft petals of flesh were warm and wet, waiting for him. She shuddered to his probing, panting as though she'd run the length of the beach; Cal swiftly dealt with one of the foil envelopes. And then, at last, Marnie felt him thrust within her, joined to her in the most intimate of ways. She opened her eyes, wrapping her arms around him, moving her hips instinctually as she spiraled into the eddies of a river she'd never traveled, drowning in the whiteness of foam.

She said his name, once, twice, and felt his inner throbbing join her own, heard his voice cry out, husky with pain and deep pleasure as he emptied within her. I love you, she thought. The way I'm feeling must be love. What else could be so overwhelming and complete?

He collapsed on top of her, his chest heaving, his breath wafting over her bare shoulder. "Darling Marnie," he whispered. "You feel so good, so right to me, I never want to let you go."

"Then don't," she murmured, rubbing her palms gently across the broad expanse of his back. He held her close, the hard pounding of his heart gradually slowing, her own blood quietening in her veins. Just like a waterfall loses itself in a deep pool, thought Marnie, and said, "I'm glad I've never made love with anyone but Terry...that I waited for you." She wrinkled her nose. "I must've known about you somehow."

"I must've been doing something right to deserve you," Cal said, scattering little kisses all over her face before burying his face in her hair. "You smell so nice," he mumbled.

"Not as nice as you," she said with such artless enthusiasm that laughter quivered in his chest.

"So when, dearest Marnie, did you decide you didn't want Pierrot doing the cooking?"

"Last night. And when I woke up this morning, I knew I was right. It was only when you arrived that I got scared." She ran her fingers along his forearm, admiring the way ligament, muscle and bone were so smoothly interwoven, loving the warmth of his skin. So close. So much hers. As she nuzzled her face into his shoulder, she added, "I bet I could pick you out from a dozen men with my eyes closed."

"After what we just did, you're talking about eleven other men?" he complained, brushing his palm lightly over her nipple. "I can see I'll have to prove I've got more to offer than the rest of them."

"Besides," she added determinedly, "the date we'd planned sounded altogether too predictable—Cal, what are you doing to me?"

"Counteracting, I trust, any tendency to boredom."

"You're doing a fantastic job."

"Good." As he took the tip of her breast in his mouth

with exquisite gentleness, he must have felt her shiver in response. Taking his time, savoring each inch of her, Cal slid lower on her body, his hair black as night against the pallor of her skin. Then he eased her thighs apart. Marnie gave a startled moan of pleasure as he found all her sensitivities, playing with her until she was arched beneath him and the inexorable rhythms made her cry out his name in a broken voice she scarcely recognized as her own.

As he raised his head, she drew him to her, lost in a sensual haze of surrender. "I never knew it could be like that," she murmured, knowing she was on the verge of tears. "So sweet... Hold me, Cal, please."

"Don't cry, sweetheart. I only want you to be happy."

"I couldn't be any happier," Marnie said with obvious sincerity, plunking her head down on his shoulder with a sigh of fulfillment. "I'm adding another word to my vocabulary," she went on drowsily. "Besides erotic, I mean. Intimacy. Being in bed with you like this has got to be the most intimate thing I've ever done in my entire life."

She'd been up late the night before and early this morning; her lashes drifted to her cheeks and her breathing deepened. So she missed the look on Cal's face, a look of mingled amusement, satiation, happiness and panic.

When Marnie awoke, she wondered for a moment if she was dreaming. She was in bed, her own bed, Cal's hands molding her curves to the hard planes of his chest; he was caressing the fullness of her breasts, smiling at her with a tenderness that melted her heart within her. Her whole body ached with desire; more than anything else in the world she wanted to give as much pleasure to Cal as he'd already given her.

Shyly at first, then with increasing boldness, Marnie took the initiative, discovering what pleased him, with secret delight watching the changing expressions on his face as she experimented in a freedom that was beyond any fantasies she could possibly have conceived. The end result was, of course, entirely predictable: a storm of passion that caught both of them in its coils and tossed them, breathless, back on the bed.

"Oh my goodness," Marnie gasped, and gave him a dazzled smile.

With sudden passionate intensity, Cal said, "You free me, Marnie. You let me be myself."

Again, tears blurred her vision. "I'm glad," she whispered, touched to the core. "I'm so glad."

"I knew from the first moment we met that I wanted to make love to you, but I never thought it could be as—hell, I don't even know what words to use."

"Maybe because there aren't any," she said with an air of discovery. "Maybe there are times our bodies have to speak for us."

"I have the feeling you've just said something very profound," Cal said, not entirely joking.

"I aim to please." Marnie put her arms around him with a sigh of contentment. "This is a lot better than Pierrot's."

"That's the understatement of the year," Cal murmured, resting his cheek on her arm and closing his eyes. Within moments, he was fast asleep.

His face in repose fascinated her: the small cleft in his chin, the bump on his nose, the white scar over his eye—all so well known to her. *Could* she have fallen in love with Cal so quickly and so completely?

In rock climbing, the whole point was not to fall, or if you did, to do so safely. Was she safe to love Cal? Or was it too late to even worry about it?

He'd treated her with generosity, sensitivity and undoubted tenderness; but he'd never mentioned the word love.

And what about Kit? Kit certainly didn't love her.

Kit and Cal came as a unit.

Don't do this, Marnie, she told herself. Cal's here with you now, and that's what counts. You're the one who doesn't want your life to be too predictable. So quit worrying and enjoy what you've got.

She ran her fingers lightly down the side of his face and sank down beside him, warmed by his body, knowing this was where she belonged.

CHAPTER TWELVE

CAL didn't sleep for long. When he opened his eyes, he said with that gleam of laughter that Marnie loved, "So I wasn't dreaming...." and followed the dip of her waist with one hand, his other going to her breast. She had, against her thigh, all the evidence she needed that he was quite ready to make love with her all over again.

Blushing, she said, "I'm hungry. Why didn't any of the gothic novels I used to read have a heroine whose stomach growled when the hero kissed her?"

"Is that a hint?" Cal said, and kissed her with entrancing thoroughness.

"Lemon meringue pie, Cal," she said, her eyes dancing.

"Christine's trout."

"I'm not sure I've got the energy to put dinner on the table."

"So I've worn you out. Did you like it, Marnie?"

"Oh, yes," she said fervently, and watched his face break into laughter and what was surely happiness as well.

Eventually, they did get up, Marnie putting her robe on and shaking out her tousled curls, Cal pulling on his trousers and shirt, leaving the shirt buttons undone. With frequent pauses for kisses that ranged from playful to passionate, they ate chips and dip and drank wine while Cal barbecued the trout on Marnie's deck, where a sliver of moon was rising over the restless waves of the sea. Sitting at her pine table by the window, the roses in a vase, they ate and talked and held hands and laughed some more.

Cal was happy. Marnie was convinced of it.

And he loved her lemon meringue pie.

She made coffee, which they drank sitting very close to

each other on the chesterfield. Marnie had lit the candle; it flickered over Cal's features as he told her about his upbringing and his adventurous parents, who had drowned while rafting in the Arctic when he was only seven. "So I was brought up by my mother's brother and his wife. Very staid, very safe, boarding school as soon as I turned twelve, holidays at canoe camps and Boy Scout camps.... Oh, they were good to me in their way and I'm sure they loved me. But I was also a duty to them, one they'd have been happier without. They were a self-sufficient couple."

He paused, his expression pensive. Marnie said noncommittally, "It sounds very lonely. You've had a lot of losses, Cal—your parents, Jennifer, even the fact you couldn't father your own child."

He moved his shoulders restively. "I love Kit as if she were my own."

"I know you do. She's very lucky." Anyone who had Cal's love would be lucky, Marnie decided, and didn't pursue that thought.

"I just wish she'd...but we agreed we weren't going to talk about Kit, didn't we?" He drained his coffee. "The way I was brought up is probably why I fell for Jennifer. She was so warm and loving. It was only as the marriage progressed that I realized she was hooked into safety like my aunt and uncle."

In a low voice, Marnie asked, "Do you still love Jennifer, Cal?" She hadn't known she was going to ask that; tensely, she waited for his reply.

He pushed a chestnut strand back from her cheek, his face somber. "She'll always be a part of me, Marnie, and that's as it should be. Because of her health problems and her inability to have children, we went through some rough times together in our marriage. She was a good mother, although sometimes we argued because I felt she had a tendency to overprotect Kit." He frowned. "I'm not doing a very good job here, am I? I have so many happy memories of times Jennifer and I shared, times full of love. But if you're asking if I'm still in love with her, then the answer's no.''

He added with sudden urgency, "Let's go back to bed. I don't think I should stay overnight in case Kit phones early in the morning. But I want to hold on to you again. Right now. Because you're right—there are things we can say with our bodies that I don't have the words for.''

Things like, I love you? "All right,'' Marnie said.

As Cal stood up, he put his arms around her. "We're in deep waters. You and I and Kit.''

"A 5.11 climb.''

"I don't even want to know what that is,'' he said with a grin that was almost normal. "I climbed up a lighthouse once, a very short and stubby little lighthouse, and thought for a while I was going to have to spend the rest of my days up there.''

"I'm glad you managed to get down,'' Marnie said, batting her lashes at him. "Or we wouldn't have met.''

"Or I wouldn't be making love to you again,'' he said, and suited action to words.

Marnie had a very hard time getting out of bed the next morning. In her bathroom mirror, she looked just like a woman who'd had too little sleep the night before; some of the wonderment of Cal's embraces still seemed to linger in her eyes. Christine, for one, would know right away what Marnie had been up to.

She couldn't let any of her students guess.

She put on mascara, rather a lot of eyeshadow and a glossy lipstick, along with an orange silk blouse and olive green pants. Her toenails were still purple. Oh, well, she'd never been impressed by perfection.

She'd hated Cal's leaving the night before, she remembered, still gazing at herself in the mirror. It had been somewhere around three in the morning when he'd finally gone.

While it was some comfort to her that he'd been as reluctant to leave as she'd been to see him go, her bed had been distressingly lonely without him.

He'd had to go. Because of Kit.

Staring into the turquoise depths of her eyes, Marnie knew she'd finally discovered what it meant to make love. What was the old cliché? That the earth had moved? She'd been so ravished, so overwhelmed, that the entire universe could have moved.

Certainly she'd changed in some radical way. Never again would she belong fully to herself. Part of her was Cal's now, this man who'd brought her felicity beyond belief. *Had* she fallen in love?

Marnie didn't know. In the cool morning light, she rather thought not. Falling in love was supposed to be rapturous, exhilarating and joyful. What she felt—listening to the waves lave the empty shoreline—was frightened. As frightened as when she'd realized at the age of sixteen that she was pregnant.

What had Cal said? "Once we make love, Marnie, there's no going back."

He was right. What had happened to her was irrevocable. Cal, in putting his seal on her body, had laid claim to her soul. So much so that a fifty-miles-apart affair was out of the question. Yet what other kind of affair could she have with Cal? Kit hadn't changed. Showed no signs of changing.

If she fell in love with Cal, it could destroy her.

With an impatient sigh, Marnie picked up the lemon meringue pie, which she planned to leave in the staff room for the teachers, and went to school. A shipment of books had come, some exactly what she'd ordered, others belonging to a school that, according to the label, was in Saskatchewan. Almost glad of the mix-up, Marnie got to work. She stayed away from the staff room at noon, going home for lunch; when she got back, she didn't even blush when Christine said how well she looked. At three that afternoon, she had a gang of kids from grade eight in the library trying to make up their minds which novels to choose for book reports. This was a part of her job Marnie enjoyed, and it was a tribute to her skills that when the final bell rang, there wasn't a concerted rush for the door.

As she signed out paperbacks for a couple of the boys, something made her glance up. A girl was standing in the doorway, a haversack slung over one shoulder, her face tense: a red-haired girl in jeans and a purple sweatshirt. It was Kit.

Marnie's nerves gave an agitated leap, and it was only with an effort of will that she smothered the remembrance of how she'd spent most of the night in Kit's father's arms. Had Kit guessed? Is that why she was here?

Marnie said with admirable poise, "Hello, Kit...can you hold on? I'll be through in a few minutes."

Kit slouched into the room, ignoring the stares of three of the boys who were clearly taken with her mop of red curls. One of the girls looked from Marnie to Kit and back again, opening her mouth to say something.

Marnie said smoothly, "Here you go, Alicia, this is the book you wanted. You'd better hurry. You wouldn't want to miss the bus."

Alicia shut her mouth, took the book and left the room. The boys trailed after her. Marnie got up, feeling at a disadvantage behind her desk.

"Would you like to come home with me?" she said in a neutral voice. "It's only just down the road."

Kit nodded. She had yet to smile.

"We'll go out the side door," Marnie suggested. That way, none of the other teachers would meet Kit and see the resemblance between the two of them.

Within ten minutes, she and Kit had reached the house. Marnie felt as though Cal's presence was in every corner of the room, and she could only hope the girl was oblivious to atmosphere. Kit was looking around with thinly disguised curiosity. The little house, Marnie thought wryly, was as different from the sprawling bungalow on the cove as it could be.

"Would you like some pop, Kit? I'm addicted to chips. You can have any flavor you like."

Kit nodded again. She looked as nervous as Marnie felt, which made Marnie feel minimally better. She poured out two glasses of Coke, opened a package of barbecued chips and went back into the living room.

"Does your dad know where you are?" she asked, trying very hard not to sound too parental.

Kit said in a rush, "He thinks I'm in school…the teachers were only away for the morning. I skipped out after French class and got the Halifax bus. It stops just up the road from your school." She buried her nose in her glass.

"I don't want him to be worrying about you."

Kit raised her head. She had a little mustache of Coke and looked both defiant and heartbreakingly young. She cried, "You can't take my mother's place!"

Marnie's lashes flickered. "I wouldn't even try to do that, Kit. It would be very wrong of me. No one can take her place. And no one should."

Momentarily, Kit looked surprised by the adamance of Marnie's reply. Then she went on the attack again. "If your mother really did take me away from you, she must have hated you. Why did she?"

Wincing as much from Kit's lack of subtlety as from the question itself, Marnie answered, "That's something I've asked myself over and over again. You see, years ago, my father left her for another woman and we never saw him again. I don't even know where he is. That caused a lot of gossip in the town. My mother and I were never close. She was too busy being the mill owner, the most powerful person in Conway Mills. Then I got pregnant after a high school dance. My turn to disgrace her. So she made sure I wouldn't go home with a baby by putting you up for adoption. I guess what I'm trying to say is that, for her, position and pride came before love.''

Her voice was low; recounting even that much of her youth still had the power to hurt.

"My mum loved me," Kit said with an edge of defiance.

Marnie met her eyes. "Then you were fortunate to have each other, even if it was for such a short time. Far too short."

In another tumble of words, Kit said, "I spent last night at Lizzie's house. Lizzie's dad is my dad's best friend, and Lizzie's mum's real neat." Kit paused for a moment. "I had to tell someone—I felt mad at the whole world, like I'd bust if I didn't let it out. So I told Lizzie's mum. She listened really hard, said she knew someone once who sounded just like your mum and perhaps I should give you the benefit of the doubt."

The phrase was obviously a direct quote. Sending up a private prayer of thanks to Lizzie's mum, Marnie said, "I'm glad you confided in her."

"Dad said I shouldn't tell anyone."

"If Lizzie's parents are such good friends, I doubt he'd mind."

"Lizzie's mum said if Dad believed your story, then probably I should, too."

"But you don't," Marnie said dryly.

"I don't know!"

Marnie would have much preferred that Kit believe her outright. She said, feeling her way, "I'm glad you came here, Kit. And that you're being so honest with me. Maybe that's enough to go on for now. On the weekend, you'll meet Terry and your grandparents, and we'll just have to see what happens."

Kit chomped on a mouthful of chips. "I had to tell you about not taking my mum's place. I don't know why, but I just had to," she said vehemently.

"I do understand." Oddly enough, Marnie did. And although she wanted nothing more than to take Kit in her arms, she knew better than even to touch her.

Kit gave her a look compounded equally of distrust and conjecture. Marnie bore it bravely, then said, "Maybe you should give your dad a call."

"He'll be mad," Kit said philosophically, and picked up the phone. The conversation at her end was brief. Replacing the receiver, she said, "He'll be here in an hour."

Marnie said, "Would you like to see a photo of Terry and his parents?"

"I—I guess so."

Marnie passed over the photo from her bookshelves, her heart aching as she saw how voraciously Kit's gaze roamed over the four faces. She talked for a while about how good Marylou and Dave had been to her and about some of the outings she'd had with her surrogate family. Kit said little, but Marnie could tell she was listening; that in itself was a big step. Then they went for a walk on the beach, joining up with Midnight. Marnie was delighted to see Kit forget her dignity, chasing after the dog and screeching in dismay when she got splashed with cold ocean water. Eventually, Marnie said, "We'd better go back. Your dad should be here soon."

Kit's face lost some of its animation. She scuffed up the pebbled rise and through the trees, the breeze playing with her vivid curls. As they both went indoors and Marnie poured more pop in their glasses, Kit said, "Dad told me you go rock climbing."

Marnie nodded. "I started about five years ago."

"Our gym class had a minicourse on the university wall. But I never did it again."

"Did you like it?"

"It was scary and fun. Both. I tease Dad, tell him the reason we have a bungalow is so he won't have to go upstairs."

Marnie chuckled. "Different strokes for different folks."

Kit picked at the hem of her sweatshirt. "Maybe it's hereditary," she said. "Me liking it, I mean."

Marnie's smile faded. Tears pricked at her lids. She said unsteadily, "Maybe it is," and heard a vehicle turn down her driveway. She blinked hard, adding, "Sounds like your father."

"Yeah," Kit said, and braced herself.

Marnie went to the door. Cal was loping down the slope, a tall, black-haired man wearing cords and a plaid shirt, a man who'd brought her infinite delight only hours ago. She said with artificial brightness, "Hi, Cal."

His eyes roamed her face with some of the same intensity with which his hands had roamed her body. "You okay?"

"Of course," she said. "Come on in, Kit's inside."

As she preceded him through the door, Kit stood up. "Hi, Dad," she said warily.

Cal went right to the point. "If you'd told me you wanted to see Marnie, I'd have brought you here."

Kit stood a little taller, suddenly looking more than her age. "But I needed to do this on my own."

"To see Marnie, you mean?"

"To tell her something. I just had to, Dad!"

Cal, Marnie noticed, didn't ask what it was that his daughter had needed to say. "I'm glad at least that you came on the bus. That you didn't try hitchhiking."

A gamine grin lit up Kit's face. "Hey, I didn't want to be grounded for life."

"So are you done?"

Kit looked over at Marnie, who was standing like a stick at the door. With the volatility that Marnie was already recognizing as very much part of her daughter, Kit's face clouded. "She'll never take **Mum's place**," she said fiercely. "That's what I had to tell her."

Cal's mouth tightened; a flash of sheer agony whipped across his face and was gone so quickly Marnie wondered if she'd imagined it. "Of course she won't," he said. "No one can take your mother's place."

It was Marnie's turn to feel pain as sharp as a shard of ice. If Cal was saying Jennifer had been a unique person and hence irreplaceable, she could accept that. But perhaps he was saying he had no intention of remarrying as long as Kit was under his roof, which wasn't the same thing at all.

Kit was chewing on her lip, her dark brown eyes suddenly swimming with tears. She said raggedly, "You didn't stop Mum from dying, Dad. I kept waiting for you to make it better—to make her better—and you never did."

For a moment, Cal looked as though Kit had punched him hard in the gut. "I couldn't," he said hoarsely.

"Then you should have told me you couldn't!"

"But...didn't you know?"

"I thought you could fix anything," Kit quavered. "You were my father. You'd stopped Tommy Hartling from bullying me and you'd mended my bike after I crashed it into the fence. Of course I thought you could make Mum better."

"Oh, God, Kit—"

"I was only ten years old, Dad! I knew other people died, but not my very own mother."

By now, tears were streaming down Kit's face. Marnie forced herself to stay by the door. Not by even the smallest of movements could she break into this confrontation between father and daughter: a confrontation two years overdue, unless she was badly mistaken. But she also longed to comfort Cal; he was gazing at Kit as if he'd never really seen her before, as if an abyss had opened right in front of his feet too late for him to avoid stepping into it. He said blankly, "You blamed me for her death."

"Of course I did!"

"Kit, she had cancer—"

Marnie doubted that Kit even heard him. "Who else

could I blame?'' the girl burst out. ''I couldn't blame her! Not Mum...''

As she scrubbed at her wet cheeks, her eyes wild with remembered pain, Cal walked over and put his arms around her, folding her to his chest and patting her awkwardly on the back. ''Honey, I'm so sorry...I had no idea you felt like that.''

Kit abandoned herself to a storm of sobbing, the heart-broken sobs of a child who's had to grow up too quickly. Marnie held her breath, wondering if she dared hope that this would somehow heal the rift between Kit and Cal. And couldn't healing in one direction lead to acceptance in another? Kit's acceptance of Marnie's presence in her life?

Eventually, Kit quietened, sagging in her father's embrace. Marnie brought a box of tissues from the bathroom, mentally going over the contents of her refrigerator to see what she could produce for supper. Kit's visit today had been the essence of unpredictability; but there was some lasagna in the freezer and chocolate chip cookies she could serve with ice cream.

Kit straightened, blowing her nose and scrubbing at her eyes. Then she muttered, ''Take me home, Dad.''

''Sure,'' Cal said.

''Right now...please.''

Bitterly disappointed, Marnie abandoned her plans for a family meal, a dinner for three eaten at her pine table overlooking the sea. She, Kit and Cal weren't a family. And home for Kit was where Jennifer had lived, the lovely bungalow on the cove. Hoping her face didn't show her feelings, she watched Cal drop a kiss on his daughter's cheek. He said, ''I'm really glad you told me all that, Kit.''

''Yeah...let's go.''

Kit couldn't wait to be gone, Marnie thought with another nasty jab at her heart. Once again, she, Marnie, was the outsider, the one left alone without a real family of her own. Subconsciously, she now realized, she'd been hoping that the events of the afternoon would somehow issue in an invitation to watch Kit play basketball at the tournament this weekend. To go public with the resemblance between the two of them. To play an ordinary role in her daughter's life.

Kit clearly didn't want any such thing.

Oh, give it up, she berated herself. Self-pity's a yucky emotion. Get a grip, Marnie. She said with a casualness that almost rang true, "Kit, I hope you'll come back— you're welcome here any time."

"Thanks," Kit mumbled.

Cal had to have heard the withdrawal in Kit's voice and to have seen the way his daughter was looking anywhere but at Marnie. All of a sudden, he looked utterly exhausted, as though he'd dug a dozen wells in a faraway country under the blazing sun only to discover there was no water. "Let's go, Kit," he said.

Kit hurried up the driveway. But as she climbed in the Cherokee, Cal pivoted and jogged back to the house. Her heart thumping, Marnie held the screen door open.

Standing outside, in a way that seemed symbolic to Marnie, Cal said choppily, "We've got to talk—figure out how we're going to handle all this. I'll give you a call later this evening." He made, of course, no move to touch her. No one, least of all Kit, would have suspected that he'd spent the better part of eight hours in Marnie's bed the night before, making passionate love to her.

It didn't take a genius in human relations to see that he was regretting that particular move. That he'd heard Kit's avowal that Marnie could never replace Jennifer; that his daughter came first and Marnie a faraway second. Once, what seemed like a very long time ago, Marnie had told Cal he was a good father. Could she now fault him for putting his daughter first? Kit had been part of his life for nearly thirteen years, Marnie for less than a month.

No contest, she thought, and in a flare of mingled terror and perversity said, "I'm going out tonight."

"Then I'll get hold of you tomorrow."

"Mario and I are climbing at Paces Lake tomorrow."

"So you've got time for Mario and not for me?"

"You've no reason in the world to be jealous of Mario!"

Cal said in a tight voice, "You're acting as if we never slept together last night. Or didn't that mean a damn thing to you?"

It had meant entirely too much. "Whereas you're wishing we'd gone to Halifax and seen a movie."

"I've got a twelve-year-old daughter who doesn't want you in her life. What the hell am I supposed to do?"

"I have no idea," Marnie said with the calm of despair. "Hadn't you better go? She'll be wondering what's up."

The words wrenched from him, he said, "You and I— we made love last night."

"Did we, Cal? Did we really?" Marnie asked and, as soon as the words were out of her mouth, wished them unsaid.

A muscle twitched in his jaw; for a few seconds that felt as long as an hour to Marnie, he was silent. Then he rasped, "If you're not going to be home, then I'll have to leave a message on your machine, won't I?" and strode back up the driveway to his vehicle.

He hadn't answered her question. Trying to dredge up anger to mask a mixture of fear and pain, Marnie watched his tires churn up the dirt as he accelerated. However, she couldn't make herself feel angry; she only felt hurt.

The Cherokee rocketed out of sight. Marnie closed the door, her thoughts carrying her forward with a logic she abhorred and an honesty she couldn't deny. Cal was the one who'd suggested last weekend that they cool it as far as touching, kisses and sex were concerned. Cal was the one who hadn't brought any protection on Wednesday night so he wouldn't be tempted to take her to bed. It was she who'd instigated the lovemaking. Not Cal. She who'd given herself body and soul to a man whose daughter hated her.

She'd been a fool.

Living dangerously sometimes meant the dangers caught up with you. Cal, she was convinced, now believed he should have stayed fifty miles away from her bed. Away from her.

Her living room looked unbearably empty, and the view of rocks and ocean only increased her sense of isolation, a deep loneliness of the spirit that brought agonizingly to life those first few months after the adoption.

She'd made love with Terry and then lost Kit. And now she'd made love with Cal and lost him, too—because of Kit.

They should have eaten at Pierrot's after all.

CHAPTER THIRTEEN

MARNIE chewed away at a peanut butter and cheese spread sandwich for supper, a sticky mixture that suited her mood. Because she'd told Cal she was going out, she went for a long walk on the beach, then drove to the nearest takeout for a double ice-cream cone, bubble gum delight on the bottom and moon mist on top. Neither flavor brought her any comfort. Back at the house, her answering machine indicated no one had phoned her. She said a very rude word and went to bed.

The next day, Marnie left for the cliffs at Paces Lake right after work. She and Mario tackled the climb known as the Pyramid, an undertaking that claimed every bit of her attention and energy. She acquitted herself admirably. When she got home, the green light was flashing by her telephone.

She was tired and horribly depressed and badly in need of a hot bath. She pushed the button and heard Cal's voice surge into the room. "I loathe answering machines," he snarled, "but you didn't leave me any choice, did you? Marnie, it must be as clear to you as it is to me that Wednesday night shouldn't have happened. I thought I could keep you and Kit separate, but I can't. You and I are adults, but Kit's not yet thirteen—she's my responsibility. I have to put her first. Surely you can see that? I knew I was right when I said we should cool it. But I let my body overrule my brain...dammit to hell, you don't know how much I hate this. We'll pick you up tomorrow afternoon around three. And, for God's sake, don't play any more games with me. I'm not up for it.''

The connection was cut with an abruptness that suggested he'd slammed the receiver down.

Marnie did likewise. Anger was safer than tears; and safety was going to be her motto from now on. No more risks. No more opening her arms and her body to a man who could repudiate her forty-eight hours later. On an answering machine, of all things. How dare he tell her that a lovemaking that had shaken her to the soul had been nothing but a mistake?

Of course, if she'd stayed home, she could have talked to him herself.

With a toss of her red curls, Marnie went to have a bath. As she soaked in a froth of raspberry bubbles, she admitted to herself that she was embracing anger with the same fervor with which she'd embraced Cal because she was dreading the weekend. To go back to Conway Mills was bad enough. To face Terry, Marylou and Dave in the company of Kit was even worse. But worst of all would be spending two days with Cal.

The only bright spot was that they wouldn't even for a minute find themselves alone.

Two whole days. It would be awful. Absolutely awful.

The water gurgled down the drain. Marnie went to bed, where she dreamed that she and Cal were discovered in a flagrantly compromising position by the Faulkner Beach Ladies' Aid. Whereupon Cal turned into a judge in a red robe and a curled wig, who handed her down a life sentence of solitary confinement. When she woke up with a start, it took her a moment or two to orient herself, to discover that she was safe in her own bed. Not on the way to prison.

The compromising position, she realized with burning cheeks, was one she and Cal hadn't actually tried.

Not that she cared. She was never going to bed with Cal Huntingdon again.

At eight-thirty on Saturday evening, Cal drove into the small town of Conway Mills. Kit was asleep in the back seat; she had, according to Cal, played three brilliant games at the tournament and was largely responsible for her team's winning the trophy for their league. She'd told none of this to Marnie; to Marnie's infinite discouragement, Kit had retreated into adolescent taciturnity again, just as though she'd never visited the little house by the sea and played with Midnight on the beach.

Cal, since his message on Marnie's machine the night before, had obviously decided on a strategy to deal with her. Throughout the whole drive, he'd been polite, distant and discreet. As if they were two strangers meeting for the first time and in no way drawn to each other, or as if she meant nothing to him at all, Marnie thought. She was almost glad because it nourished her anger and kept at bay a pain that would overwhelm her if she allowed it entry.

He asked now, "How do I get to Dave and Marylou's?"

"Keep going straight. Not many choices in Conway Mills," Marnie said, trying very hard to relax her hands in her lap. In the twilight, the houses clustered around the few stores looked secretive and unwelcoming. As they turned the corner by the two churches, she added, "That driveway goes up to my mother's house...you can see it through the trees."

As Cal slowed, she caught sight of the tall-paned windows arrayed like empty eyes below the black expanse of the roof. She shivered, wishing she was anywhere else but here.

"Dave's house is around the next corner. It's painted pink and green—Marylou's always liked bright colors."

Cal said nothing. If she was tense, she thought with reluctant empathy, so was he. Not about her, of course. Oh, no, he'd turned her off like the kitchen tap. Cal, she was almost sure, was worried sick about the imminent meeting between Kit and Terry, the man whose genes Kit bore. The only other man with whom Marnie had made love.

Cal turned into the driveway, which led through a double row of maples to an old farmhouse surrounded by budding lilacs and the rosy sunsets of quince bushes in full bloom. As though he'd been waiting for them to arrive, a man came around the corner of the house, a tall man with a thatch of light brown hair and deep brown eyes. Marnie's catch of breath wasn't lost on Cal. He demanded flatly, "Is that Terry?"

She nodded, quite unable to find her voice. Quickly, she unlatched her seat belt and got out of the Cherokee. If Terry's grin was a shade less ebullient than usual, she was in no shape to notice. He picked her up and lifted her above his head, then deposited her on the ground, hugged her and kissed her warmly on both cheeks. "Hiya, Mar," he said.

"Hi, yourself." She gave him a credible smile. "You look great."

"You get more gorgeous all the time. Old age agrees with you." Then he looked past her. "You must be Cal. I'm Terry Dyson."

The two men shook hands, Cal's slate blue eyes cool and watchful. Marnie babbled, "Kit slept the whole way, she played in a basketball tournament yesterday and today and she probably...oh, here she is."

Kit was standing by the Cherokee, the setting sun falling on her crop of bright curls and on the brown eyes that were so like Terry's. For once, Marnie saw that Terry was at a loss for words. He took a couple of steps toward Kit and said stiffly, "I'm Terry...you must be Kit." The girl nodded, and for a few seconds that felt like hours to Marnie, the two of them simply stared at each other. Marnie was about to say something—anything—to break the silence when Terry added in a stilted voice, "How are you?"

"Okay."

The rigidity of her stance made a liar out of her; Terry said with something approaching a smile, "That's got to be the stupidest question I've ever asked. If you're feeling anything like me, you don't have a clue how to behave or what to say. This isn't exactly your average everyday occurrence, is it? Maybe sometime tomorrow you and I could go for a walk and get to know each other a bit…if you feel like it."

"That'd be neat," Kit said.

"Great. Let's go in and you can meet my mum and dad. We might as well get all the introductions over and done with and then perhaps we can start acting like normal human beings."

The two of them started up the front steps side by side. Marnie stole a look at Cal. He was staring after them, his face inscrutable, his fists clenched at his sides. She forgot that she was angry with him and that she'd vowed to play it safe, and said softly, "Cal, you'll always be Kit's dad no matter how much time she spends with Terry."

He looked at her, his gaze turbulent as a summer storm. "He sure kissed you as if you're more than good friends."

"He didn't and we aren't."

"Who'd you go out with on Thursday night, Marnie?"

"I had a heavy date with a bubble gum ice-cream cone," she seethed, "and we can't start a fight now, not when you're about to meet Kit's grandparents. Anyway, there's nothing to fight about—you said it all very comprehensively on my answering machine."

"And whose fault was it I had to use that goddamned machine?"

"Am I supposed to sit home night after night waiting for you to call?" she retorted with complete unfairness.

"You chickened out, didn't you?" he rasped. "You went out for a stupid ice-cream cone so you wouldn't have to talk to me on the phone. I never thought you were a coward, Marnie."

"Then you don't know me very well."

"I know you all too well," he grated, his eyes raking her from head to foot in her pretty flared dress. Then he took the front steps two at a time and held the screen door open for her.

She found herself staring at his hand on the door, a hand that had explored her body with an intimacy she'd adored. "I should never have canceled Pierrot's," she whispered. "Everything's gone wrong since then. The trouble is, I was silly enough to believe you when you said you liked living dangerously."

"There's danger and there's total irresponsibility," Cal snarled.

He couldn't have said anything more calculated to hurt. Deep down, Marnie was beginning to believe she had been irresponsible to make love with Kit's father; she must have been because look at the results. With the truth of despair, she said, "I'd hoped I could have both of you...was that so wrong of me? But instead, I don't have either one. At least you have Kit."

Then she walked past him to join the others in the kitchen.

Saturday night and Sunday were never very clear in Marnie's memory. Dave and Marylou made everyone feel more than welcome, Dave's kindness being of the gruff variety, Marylou's full of chatter and delicious meals. Because both of them seemed to take it for granted that Kit would be as delighted to meet them as they were to meet her, Kit unbent almost instantly, following them around like a puppy anxious for attention. Dave and Cal took the boat early Sunday morning and went fishing on the river. Kit and Terry went for their walk, and on their return played basketball for a couple of hours, passing and feinting around the net that was attached to the side of the barn.

Marnie had hidden herself on the old wooden swing on the oak tree, where as a young girl she'd always taken her troubles and worries. Through the screen of pink-and-white buds decorating Dave's small orchard, she watched Kit and Terry play together, hearing their shouts of laughter with a bittersweet pleasure. Terry had always had the ability to charm the birds from the trees. Why should she be surprised that Kit wasn't immune?

Kit was certainly immune to her.

Cal hadn't invited her to go fishing. He was avoiding her like some particularly noxious weed: something deadly poisonous that made you froth at the mouth and fall down in fits and messily die.

The bolts creaked as Marnie swung back and forth. Despite the way Kit was ignoring her, she shouldn't be feeling so unhappy. Kit had listened carefully last night to Dave's laconic opinions and Marylou's much wordier ones about Charlotte Carstairs, none of which could be construed as positive. And even in this short time, Kit was forming bonds with Terry, Dave and Marylou: with her roots.

But Marnie was unhappy. The reason, of course, was Cal. It was taking every ounce of her pride, courage and just plain cussedness to get through this weekend, through the frustration and pain of being so close to him and yet so infinitely far away.

Restlessly, she got up from the swing and went into the house. Marylou, despite her talkativeness, also knew when to be quiet; after one look at the shadows under Marnie's eyes, she passed her the rolling pin and put her to work. By the time Marnie had put together two rhubarb pies and made a big batch of tea biscuits, she was feeling slightly less frayed around the edges. Nothing like the aroma of pastry browning in the oven to soothe heartache, she thought, and smiled almost naturally at Terry and Kit as they tumbled through the back door, both of them sweating profusely.

She poured glasses of cold apple juice and doled out hot biscuits smothered in homemade jam, not noticing that Cal and Dave were approaching the house. Waving a biscuit in the air, Kit burbled, "Terry's a real good player. He showed me a way to dribble that's pure dynamite! You wait till I try it out on our coach—oh, hi, Dad, did you catch anything?"

Cal glanced from Kit to Terry. "Two small salmon that we put back."

His big body had a stillness that Marnie recognized: the stillness that hid emotion. Terry wiped jam from his chin and said with unusual seriousness, "You've got one neat kid here, Cal. You're a lucky guy."

Kit looked from one to the other of them, her own smile fading. "Dad, will you come outside after, so I can show you what Terry taught me?"

Tensely, Marnie waited for Cal's reply to what was by no means a simple question. But Cal rose to the occasion in a way that made her proud of him, she who had no claim on him whatsoever. He said easily, "Sure, I'd like that, Kit," and ruffled her hair. "Did you leave me any of those biscuits, you and Terry, or have you scoffed the lot?"

Kit grinned at him, a grin compounded of relief and mischief. "You'll spoil your appetite for lunch," she said primly.

"I'll risk it," Cal said, and slathered a biscuit with butter and jam. "These are great—you've been busy, Marylou."

"Oh, Marnie made the biscuits and the pies," Marylou said.

Cal winced, Marnie turned away to wash the dishes, and Dave said, "Bugs are awful bad on the river this year."

The afternoon dragged by. But finally it was time to leave. After a round of goodbyes, Marnie settled herself in the back seat and, as soon as they'd driven onto the road, closed her eyes. She didn't wake until Cal was jouncing over the potholes in her driveway. Sitting up, she said stupidly, "We're back already?"

Cal's eyes met hers in the rearview mirror. "You slept the whole way. I'll get your bag."

Marnie said rapidly, "Bye, Kit. I'm glad you had a good time."

"See you," Kit said.

A meaningless phrase if ever there was one, Marnie thought, and scrambled out of her seat, hoping she'd make it into the house before she started to cry. Whenever she'd imagined a reunion with her daughter, she'd pictured the two of them falling into each other's arms in mutual delight. Reality had sure put paid to that particular scenario.

Cal had taken her bag out of the back. Marnie took it gingerly, knowing if he touched her she'd fall apart in the driveway. "Thanks for doing all the driving," she said politely. "I hope you're not too tired."

"Are you going to Sandy Lake next Friday?" he demanded.

Friday began the long weekend when she and Christine usually went camping at Sandy Lake Park, and Cal and Kit did, too. Not on your life, Marnie thought, and said coolly, "Probably not. Some friends are going to Cape Breton to rock climb. I expect that's what I'll do."

"Marnie, we can't go on like this. I'll phone you through the week and—"

"No, don't," she gasped. "You mustn't. You were right, we made a terrible mistake. Goodbye, Cal."

She hurried down the slope to her front door. By the time she'd inserted the key in the lock, the Cherokee was back on the highway. She stepped inside, locked the door firmly behind her and stared in blind misery at the restless waves of the sea.

On Monday after school, Marnie told Christine she wasn't going to Sandy Lake. "Why ever not?" Chris asked.

"Mario and the crew are heading for Cape Breton and it's a great chance to—"

"Have Don and I done anything to offend you?"

"Of course not, that's—"

"Come clean, Marnie!"

"All right, all right. Cal and Kit go to Sandy Lake every year on the long weekend in May. So therefore I'm not."

"You and I have gone to Sandy Lake for the past three years. You're going to let that man break a tradition that's really important to me?"

"Are you trying to make me feel guilty?"

"You bet. Anyway, Don's brother from Toronto is coming, too. I want you to meet him. Maybe he'll take your mind off that hunk who's Kit's father."

"I wish," Marnie said.

"I could kill him," Chris said theatrically. "We'll go over the menus tomorrow and leave Friday as soon as we're packed."

So that was that. Once again, Marnie thought unhappily,

she was living dangerously. Although it was a big park and there was no real likelihood that she'd meet up with Cal and Kit.

When the four of them registered at the park headquarters on Friday evening, Marnie saw with a sinking heart that the campsite next to the one they'd be occupying Saturday and Sunday nights was assigned to a C. Huntingdon, party of two. Both campsites were near a small cliff that she'd climbed in the past and intended to climb again this weekend. It must be pure coincidence that Cal had ended up with the adjacent site because theirs was listed under Don's name, and Cal would have no reason to connect a Donald Whiteley with Marnie.

Damn Cal anyway, she thought, and signed the registration form with an angry flourish.

The two men had gone to the washroom. "What's the matter?" Christine asked with rather overdone innocence.

Marnie's eyes narrowed. "You're the one who registered us. Chris, how *could* you have put us next to Cal?"

"It was easy, actually. I just asked."

"You're pushing your luck!"

"I can't stand seeing you so miserable. Maybe you could try drowning in front of him so that he'll rush to your rescue and realize he's madly in love with you."

"Maybe you should try minding your own business."

Chris wailed, "I only want you to be happy."

Marnie, of course, wanted the same thing. But she didn't think camping next door to Cal and Kit was the way to achieve it.

They stayed on the shore that night since it was too dark by then to cross the lake. On Saturday, they paddled to their other site, which was tucked among the trees on a small peninsula, with a good breeze to keep the flies away.

Cal's campsite was quite a distance away; Marnie saw no sign of him or Kit that morning and in the afternoon did her climb.

At sunset, she and Don's brother, William, who was as chubby as Don was lean, took her canoe out on the lake. William wanted to learn some bow strokes, so Marnie steered him among the rocks, showing how the draws and pries worked. He was slashing away at the water with more enthusiasm than accuracy, Marnie steadying the canoe from the stern, when around a rim of boulders came a sleek cedar-strip canoe, the gunwale keeled over almost to water level, a man kneeling amidships; the last rays of the sun lit his bare chest and thighs with gold. His hair was black, his eyes like shadowed pits.

Marnie almost dropped her paddle. The breeze swung the bow around and William yelled, "There's a big mother of a rock straight ahead."

Hastily, Marnie did a J-stroke. Trying to look calm and unflappable, she said, "Good evening, Cal."

CHAPTER FOURTEEN

CAL brought his canoe to a swirling halt, impaling Marnie with a look of such hostility that for a moment her heart quailed. Then he transferred the hostility to William and demanded, "Is this the friend you were going climbing with in Cape Breton?"

Ridiculous, Marnie thought, a scene right out of *True Confessions*. Discovering that no matter how alienated she felt from Cal she didn't want him thinking she and William were a number, she said spiritedly, "William is my best friend Christine's fiancé's brother, who arrived from Toronto on Friday morning and who's going back to Toronto on Tuesday. He can climb in and out of a canoe. Just."

William said, "You left out the separate tents, Marnie."

"So I did. Thank you, William," Marnie said composedly.

William then glanced from Cal back to Marnie. "I gather you two know each other."

"You could say so," Cal snapped.

"Why don't I jump overboard and swim back? That way you can be alone together," William said helpfully.

"Stay put," Marnie said with ferocious emphasis. "I'm a mistake Cal made—he doesn't want anything to do with me."

"That's about as far from the truth as you're likely to hear, William," Cal snorted, sculling with his paddle to bring the two canoes closer.

"Where's Kit?" Marnie asked with a mutinous toss of her curls.

"Back at the campsite cooking supper. She's a much better basketball player than a cook, so I'm trying to work up an appetite."

Marnie was too flustered to bother with a minor detail like discretion. Giving his naked torso the once-over, she announced, "You're working up other appetites. In me. Not that that could possibly interest you."

"Wrong again," Cal said bitterly. "That particular appetite never lets up, night or day."

"But you've decided we shouldn't do anything about it."

"Marnie," Cal exploded, "Kit exists and she doesn't want you replacing her mother. You know that as well as I do. I had to back off!"

"Sex should never have been invented!"

Cal said an unprintable word, bringing his canoe around in a flurry of spray. "Nice meeting you, William. I bet you'll find Toronto dull after Sandy Lake and make bloody sure the tents stay separate."

William said with genuine amusement, "I wouldn't dare do otherwise. When are you two going to figure out that you're in love with each other?" Then, with a cherubic smile, he did a vigorous forward stroke and sailed past Cal.

"We are not!" Marnie choked, and dug her paddle into the water with vicious strength.

If Cal said anything in reply, she didn't hear it. But the image of his dark-pelted chest and narrow hips had burned itself into her brain, and a nasty combination of physical longing and sheer misery kept her awake for a long time after darkness fell. Kit was avoiding her like the plague; Cal desired her yet wished her a million miles away. No wonder she was turning into an insomniac.

But William was wrong. She wasn't in love with Cal. Or he with her.

By eight-thirty the next morning, feeling grumpy and heavy-eyed, Marnie was in the stern of her canoe attempting to show William, who was in the water, how to get back into the boat. His attempts made the canoe rock and sway. "If you dump me," she said, "I'll never let you hear the last of it—not like that, William!"

"*Marnie!*"

Marnie's head slewed around; it was Cal's voice, raw with urgency. With a jar to her nerves, she saw him standing on the beach, breathing hard as though he'd been running. He was wearing the same blue shorts he'd had on last night. She said sharply, "Let go, William," and raced her canoe to shore, jumping out into the shallows and hauling the bow up on the sand. "What's wrong?"

Cal said in a strained voice, "When I woke up this morning, I found a note from Kit saying she'd gone to climb the cliff back of the campsites, so I went over there as fast as I could. She's got herself stuck halfway up. She can't go up or down and there's no one else there. You've got to help her, Marnie."

Kit in danger. Marnie's heart gave a great thud in her chest and for a moment her throat closed with terror. "Two seconds," she gasped, then hurried to her tent. She dragged on shorts and a T-shirt over her bikini, thrust her feet into sneakers and grabbed her climbing bag. Then she backed out of the tent. "Let's go."

The two of them ran down the path, taking the narrow trail that led to the cliff, Cal in the lead. He was setting a killing pace; she wasn't sure she'd ever forget the look on his face when he told her about Kit's predicament.

Nothing must happen to Kit. Nothing.

There was a boggy area at the base of the cliff, where rhodora bloomed in purple profusion and mosquitoes bred in equal profusion. Marnie saw Kit immediately. The girl had sensibly tackled the easiest slope but had run into difficulties near an overhang and lacked the skills to go either forward or backward. She was now splayed against the rock in a position that put maximum strain on her arms and hands.

If she fell, she could do herself a lot of damage.

She's not going to fall. I won't let her.

Marnie bent to put on her climbing shoes. "Don't worry, Cal, I'll get her down from there in no time."

He said hoarsely, "I'll never forgive myself if anything happens to her. She's the one who wanted us to camp at this end of the lake—we usually go near the stillwater. She must've planned this all along. I was just too stupid to catch on."

Marnie stuck her bare foot into her second shoe. "She'll be fine. I promise."

"Last Wednesday," he went on in the same hoarse voice, "the way I felt with you in bed—it was earth-shattering, turned my whole world upside down. Scared the hell out of me. So I backed off. Yeah, it had a lot to do with Kit. But it had to do with me, as well. Being terrified of losing you if once I gave in to the way you make me feel. Just like I'm terrified of losing Kit right now."

Marnie straightened. She couldn't begin to take in what he'd just said, not when she needed all her focus on the job at hand. "We can't talk about it now," she said tightly. "I have to get Kit down as quickly as I can." It was one thing to tackle a climb on her own; quite another to rescue her own daughter. She turned her back on him, forcing herself to assess the rock face for the best route.

"Aren't you going to take any ropes?"

"No need."

"What if you fall?"

"Cal, I won't fall and neither will Kit. Trust me." Which was an all-important statement if ever there was one, she thought, and deliberately put Cal out of her mind.

Having made a decision about her route, Marnie started to climb, continually searching for holds, her body moving with confidence and a kind of elegance up the granite slope, almost as though she were an extension of the rock, a creature whose natural element was granite.

When she was within easy earshot of Kit, she called, "Hang in there—another few minutes."

Kit said nothing.

Marnie brought herself level with the girl, then traversed toward her along a ledge, crossing one foot behind the other. She smiled at Kit, who looked very relieved to see her and thoroughly ashamed of herself. Marnie said, "If you only had that one lesson, you did well to get as far as this."

Kit looked startled; plainly she'd expected a scolding. "But I shouldn't have done it."

"Probably not, especially on your own. It's only the past couple of years I've started to go solo. For starters, how about if you take a little rest?"

"My arms are aching," Kit said in a rush. "And my fingers hurt."

"That's because you're putting too much strain on them. Transfer all your weight to your left foot and really dig it into the rock. That way it'll stick. And keep your heel down—it's easier on your leg muscles that way. Bring your other foot up to that little ledge...feel it? You're doing great." Kit did as she was told, her face intent in a way Marnie found heartening. In the same easy voice, Marnie said, "Now bring your hands down one by one to the same crack I'm holding…got that? And last of all, move your hips away from the rock—that way you're balanced over your feet and legs.''

As Kit awkwardly obeyed her, her expression changed. ''Wow,'' she said, ''what a difference—I can really feel it!''

Marnie laughed. ''You're a natural. But you were making a common mistake for beginners—not letting your legs bear most of the weight. Hauling yourself up by your arms defeats the strongest of climbers.''

Kit looked over at Marnie, studying her stance. ''Your hands are down low,'' she said. ''Mine were way over my head.''

''Low works much better. Helps me to remember to look down for holds. Not up.''

''I've got a lot to learn.''

''You think I haven't?'' Marnie grinned. ''Feeling better? Ready to head back down?''

''Yeah,'' Kit said. ''Will you keep on showing me what to do? It's cool.''

''Of course I will.''

Suiting her actions to her words, Marnie began a series of calm-voiced directions, always keeping level with Kit as she pointed out possible holds, insistent that the girl keep her body in balance over the rock. When they took another short rest about halfway down, Kit said humbly, ''I'm not nearly as tired as I was—I was making some pretty dumb moves.''

''But you're willing to learn from your mistakes. Which is probably one of the most valuable assets any climber can have.''

Kit shifted her fingers, pressing her palm into the rock face as Marnie had shown her. Then she said very fast, looking straight at Marnie, "I've been a real jerk since I met you...I'm sorry."

"Oh, Kit," Marnie said helplessly.

"You're neat," Kit said. "Real neat. C'n we start over?"

"We sure can," Marnie said. "I'd like that."

Kit gave her a dazzling smile. "Great! Now we'd better get down before Dad has a heart attack."

Marnie laughed. "Right on. Why don't you see if you can find the next toehold yourself?"

Frowning in concentration, obviously going over in her head everything Marnie had told her, Kit did a creditable job with her next holds. The slope was leveling out; nevertheless, Marnie was pleased to see that Kit didn't rush the last few feet. Finally, they were both standing on flat ground. Kit turned around to face her father. "Sorry, Dad," she said.

In a cracked voice, Cal said, "You're safe," and took her in his arms.

He was white about the mouth. Considering his phobia for heights, Marnie knew it must have been torture for him to watch the two of them inching down the slope. Then Kit raised her head. "Dad," the girl said, "I want to take climbing lessons."

"Oh, God," Cal groaned.

"With Marnie, if she wants to," Kit said, her brown eyes full of pleading as she looked over her shoulder at the woman watching them.

"I'd love to teach you," Marnie said truthfully. "But it's up to your father."

Cal took a long breath and exhaled it, moving his shoulders to rid them of tension. He looked down at his daughter. "You liked that? Being stuck halfway up a cliff? Clawing your way down by your fingernails?"

"I didn't like being stuck and not knowing what to do. But Marnie showed me such a lot. It's cool, Dad. Awesome. Better than basketball."

Cal swallowed. "If you really want to, I guess you can."

Kit squeezed him hard, giving a whoop of pleasure. Then she wriggled free of his embrace and walked over to Marnie. Standing tall, she said seriously, "Thank you, Marnie."

Instinctively, Marnie knew what to do. As she held out her arms, Kit walked into them. Marnie dropped her cheek onto Kit's bright curls and closed her eyes, knowing she'd longed for this moment for nearly thirteen years, all the while never believing it could possibly happen.

By unspoken consent a few moments later, they released each other. Kit gave Marnie a wobbly smile. "When's the first lesson?"

Marnie began, "For your father's sake, maybe we should wait until…" Then her voice broke. Suddenly, it was all too much. The young girl who was her beloved daughter, with whom she was now truly reunited, and the tall, dark-haired man who for one glorious night had been her lover: both of them watching her in a sunlit clearing at the base of a granite cliff. Marnie sat down hard on a clump of blueberries, put her head on her knees and started to weep as though her heart was breaking, sobs tearing their way from her throat, her whole body shuddering with an uprush of emotion impossible to quell.

From a long way away, she heard Kit's distressed question and Cal's deep-voiced response. Then she felt him kneeling beside her, his arm going around her shoulders. She buried her face in his chest, all the tears that had been pent up for years streaming down her face and dripping onto her bare legs.

Gradually, more from exhaustion than anything else, she

quietened. Cal said gently, "Here, Kit had a couple of tissues in her pocket. Not used, she assures me, although they aren't what you'd call squeaky clean."

Marnie blew her nose, scrubbed at her face with her hands, also dirty from the climb, and finally looked up. "I'm s-sorry," she hiccuped, "I had no idea that was g-going to happen."

With adolescent awkwardness, Kit crouched beside her, her face a study in conflicting emotions. "You really do care about me, don't you? Or you wouldn't have cried like that."

"Of course I do," Marnie gulped. "It broke my heart to lose you so long ago. And to have found you again.... I've got to stop b-bawling my head off, it's nuts. Tell me to stop, Cal."

His face was very close to hers, so close she could have traced the cleft in his chin or drowned in the gray blue depths of his eyes. "Stop crying, Marnie," he said huskily. "And that's an order."

"You know how I f-feel about orders." She dragged her gaze away from him and produced a semblance of a smile for Kit. "My mother was the original sergeant major."

Kit said impulsively, "I do believe you about your mum. I know now that you didn't abandon me."

Again Marnie's vision blurred with tears. "Thanks," she whispered. "You don't know how much that means to me."

Cal swatted at a mosquito. "We don't have any bubble gum ice cream at the campsite, but we do have a couple of bags of chips. Why don't we go back and celebrate?"

"I should tell William that Kit's safe," Marnie mumbled. She felt tired out, calm and deeply happy all at the one time. Her daughter had been restored to her, righting an old and bitter wrong. Maybe, she thought dimly, she would now find it within herself to forgive her mother.

"We'll tell him first," Cal said, and lifted Marnie to her feet.

For a moment, she swayed against him, the touch of his hands and the closeness of his big body both working their usual magic. Maybe she and Cal would work out, too, now that the barriers between Kit and herself had fallen, she thought in a surge of optimism. With a lilt in her voice, she said, "I hope they're not just regular chips."

Kit giggled. "Spicy ketchup and dill."

"Lead me to them."

On the way back, they met Christine, Don and William, who'd been looking for them to find out what happened. Cal explained, then said, "We're going back to our campsite for lunch."

"Good," Christine said, and winked at Marnie.

"I'm going to give Kit rock-climbing lessons," Marnie said with an innocent smile. "See you later."

At the end of the trail, the others veered right, while she, Cal and Kit turned left. Kit said, "Do we still have to go home today, Dad?"

Marnie's heart gave an uncomfortable lurch; she'd taken it for granted that Cal and Kit would be staying until tomorrow, and that she'd have time to enjoy Kit's presence in a way totally new to her. Cal said, "Yeah...I'm going to Uganda tomorrow, Marnie, a consultation for an irrigation system. But I should be back by the middle of next week."

"I'm staying at Lizzie's," Kit said. "If we weren't leaving today, I could have a lesson with Marnie tomorrow."

Marnie stopped dead, a spruce bough brushing her bare arm. "Cal, Kit could stay with us at our campsite. I'd deliver her to Lizzie's tomorrow. If she wants to, and if you trust me with her.''

Her mouth dry, she waited for his response. If he said yes, he was acknowledging her place in Kit's life as the girl's mother; accepting that she was indeed trustworthy. A huge step, she thought, panic-stricken, wishing she hadn't asked, her heart banging against her ribs as she waited for him to say something. Anything.

He was staring at her, his expression unfathomable. Kit looked from one to the other and in a small voice said, ''I'd like that, Dad.''

Cal said slowly, ''I'd trust you with Kit, Marnie. Of course I would.''

Through an uprush of joy, Marnie heard Kit squeal, ''You mean it's all right? That means we can have our first lesson, Marnie.''

''At least I won't be around to watch,'' Cal said. He'd meant it as a joke, Marnie was sure; yet there was an undertone in his voice that put all her senses on alert. Later, she thought, I'll ask him about it later.

''There's one condition, Kit,'' she said. ''That we stop at the first ice-cream stand on the way home.''

''My favorite's cherry swirl,'' Kit said promptly.

Marnie's lashes flickered as she remembered the initial tempestuous meeting between herself and Cal. ''You can have a double,'' she said.

Cal's campsite was on a small beach, the cedar canoe drawn up on the sand. After they'd demolished a bag of chips and a bottle of ginger ale, Kit said, ''I'm going for a swim. Coming, you two?''

''I'll pass,'' Marnie said. ''I feel wiped—too much emotion, I guess.''

''I'll keep Marnie company,'' Cal said with a casualness

that didn't quite ring true, and again Marnie felt that shiver of unease.

Kit disappeared into the tent, reappearing in a business-like maillot. She dashed into the water, swimming out in a strong crawl. "She's very athletic," Marnie said, needing to break a silence that was getting on her nerves.

"Ever since she talked about blaming me for Jennifer's death, we've been getting along really well," Cal said, picking up a twig from the sand and shredding it, his profile to Marnie as he gazed out at the lake. "So I figured I was okay to go overseas this week, where it's just a short trip. I need to get away, Marnie. Today, watching the two of you on that cliff—I can't tell you how hard that was."

"Try," she said.

"I expected any minute for the two of you to fall. To be killed in front of my eyes." He was frowning, his jaw an unyielding line. "I could tell you're a good climber just by watching you—but this isn't about logic, it's about feelings. I thought I knew all about feelings after Jennifer's death. What I'm starting to understand is that I had no choice back then—I had to be with her step by step of the way. But with you, I do have a choice. I can get involved. Or I can back off."

With sudden violence, he snapped the twig into two separate pieces. "I'm like Kit, stuck somewhere. Halfway up a cliff. Not able to go up or down."

"Maybe you need to let me come and rescue you," Marnie said, watching a handful of sand trickle through her fingers.

"I'm not sure I can do that. What if I lost you like I lost Jennifer? I couldn't stand it."

So what was she supposed to say? That life is full of risk? That if nothing's ventured, nothing's gained? All the old clichés that were nevertheless full of truth, Marnie thought, and watched the tiny grains filter between her fingertips.

"Maybe if I go away, I'll figure it out," Cal said.

"I don't understand," Marnie said carefully. "Are you saying I'm important to you—other than as Kit's mother, that is?"

For the first time, he turned to look at her. "Well, of course you are."

"Of course?" she said, raising her brows. "I'm not a mind reader, Cal. And your face does inscrutable like a pro."

"We made love, Marnie! I keep telling you that."

"But you haven't touched me ever since!"

"How could I when Kit didn't want anything to do with you?"

Her temper rising, Marnie said, "As of an hour ago, Kit is no longer the issue."

He was gazing out at the far shore of the lake again. "I thought I knew what love was, until you came along. I loved Jennifer, I told you that. But what I feel for you— it's like a force of nature. Elemental. Unstoppable. Totally out of my control. Is that love, Marnie?"

"Why don't we risk finding out?" Marnie muttered, picking up another handful of sand.

He grabbed her by the wrist. "Do you feel the same way?" he said roughly. "Or am I only imagining that you do?"

She stared at his fingers. "You tear me apart," she said, "and you bring me such joy as I've never known."

She could feel the breeze teasing her hair; the sunlight lay like a sheen on her face.

Cal raised her hand to his lips, kissing her knuckles one by one. "You tear me apart, too," he said. "Tear to shreds the man I thought I knew. I'm the one who had to go overseas because my marriage was too confining. With Jennifer, I was always the strong one. There was a lot she didn't want to know—we had a huge fight after that magazine article because I hadn't told her how dangerous it could get. But you're different. You want me to be myself. No masks. The real man. I can tell you anything and everything, you said.''

As if it were scalding him, he dropped her hand. ''Let me tell you this much. I can hardly bear to think of you going up the side of a cliff or taking a canoe through the rapids. So I guess I'm the one who's a coward.''

That Cal was exposing his vulnerabilities to her made him far from a coward. Marnie said forthrightly, ''I won't stop climbing. Not for you or anyone else.''

''I'd never ask you to.''

''I'd never ask you to stay home from Uganda, either. Or Ghana, or the Sudan. Even though I'd worry about you dreadfully.''

''I was seven when my mum and dad died,'' he said moodily. ''I waved goodbye to them at the airport and I never saw them again. They didn't even find the bodies. And it was just five weeks from the time of Jennifer's diagnosis to her death.''

''You can't live in the past, Cal—even though it's scarred you,'' Marnie said passionately. ''Right this minute I'm alive, sitting beside you. What else is there but that? And you want me, I know you do.''

''Want, darling Marnie, is a totally inadequate word for the way I feel about you,'' he said with an ironic twist of his mouth. He took her chin gently in his fingers. ''Here's a loaded question. Would you have another child? My child?''

''*What*?''

''You heard.''

She gave a breathless laugh. "Yes."

"Even after all the pain Kit's birth brought you?"

Color staining her cheeks, Marnie said, "I'd love to bear your child, Cal."

"You're so brave and beautiful," he said. A smile lightened his features. "And I don't just mean your red hair."

"Auburn."

He held a strand full in the sun. "The color of fire."

"I'll miss you next week," she said with desperate truth.

"I'm probably every kind of a fool not to be proposing to you right now," he said. "Will you wait for me, Marnie? Wait until I come back? Because my gut's telling me I need to get away, even though I don't have a clue why."

"I'll wait," she said.

"Maybe you could meet me at the airport. It's an evening flight, a week from Wednesday."

"It sounds like forever," Marnie said, and felt his smile go right through her, making her whole body ache with desire.

"Don't look at me like that," he said thickly. "We've got a chaperon, remember? Your daughter and mine."

Somehow she knew this conversation was over, that Cal had said what he'd needed to say. "Lunch," she announced. "Why don't we get some lunch?"

They ate on the beach. After Kit had packed up her gear and Cal had everything else ready to load into his canoe, they walked to Marnie's campsite. Cal said goodbye to Kit. Then, while Kit was setting up her sleeping bag next to Marnie's in the tent, Cal drew Marnie back into the shelter of the trees and kissed her with such passionate single-mindedness that Marnie was trembling when he released her. He'd kissed her as though he'd never see her again, she thought with an inward shiver, but didn't share this conclusion with him.

"I'll see you at the airport," she said. "I'll paint my toenails purple."

"Right now I wish I wasn't going anywhere," he muttered, and kissed her again, his tongue laving hers, his hands roaming the length of her spine.

She wanted to throw him down on the ground and jump him. "Let me know your flight time," Marnie said faintly.

"I'll tell Andrea—that's Lizzie's mother—about the climbing lessons. Take care of yourself, won't you? I know you'll take care of Kit."

"Thank you for leaving her with me."

"Who better to leave her with? Bye, Marnie."

One last kiss and he was striding along the path as though he was being pursued. The forest swallowed him, the soft swishing of the evergreens smothering the sound of his footsteps. Marnie bit her lip to keep herself from calling him back. Ten days wasn't long, she thought stoutly. And she'd have Kit for company until tomorrow afternoon and again next weekend.

A month and a half ago, the prospect of being reunited with her daughter would have been happiness enough. Certainly what had happened today had made her marvelously happy and fulfilled, healing so many of the old wounds. But she wanted more. Along with Kit, she wanted Kit's father.

Who had, more or less, told her that he loved her. Hadn't he?

CHAPTER FIFTEEN

MARNIE went to bed at nine-thirty on Monday night, after soaking in a hot bath that felt wonderful after three nights of camping. The past twenty-four hours had been among the happiest in her life. Yesterday, she and Kit had swum, canoed and cooked together. They'd shared a tent and before falling asleep had talked for nearly an hour, the darkness perhaps giving them both courage. This morning, Kit had had a climbing lesson. And as the time passed, minute by slow minute, Marnie knew she and her daughter were building something new and infinitely precious: a brightly spanned bridge that would, she was certain, strengthen with every meeting.

With a sigh of repletion, she fell asleep.

At eleven-thirty, the telephone rang. Cal. It had to be Cal. Marnie leaped out of bed, tripped over one of her hooked rugs and grabbed the receiver. "Hello?" she croaked.

"Marnie? Marnie, are you there?"

The connection was appalling, full of crackles and spits. "Yes, it's me. Where are you?"

"Marnie? I can't hear a thing. Speak louder."

She yelled into the receiver, "I'm here, Cal!"

"Dammit, what's wrong with this phone? I called to tell you—" A series of cracks like rifle shots interrupted him, echoing down the line, making an incomprehensible jumble of his words. "...timing's terrible. I just wish I knew if you could hear me!"

"Where are you?" she shouted again. They weren't real

rifle shots; she was almost sure of that. Still, she was achingly aware of not only the thousands of miles between
them but also the other distances that weren't a matter of
mere geography.

Amid a volley of miniature explosions, the line went
dead. With a moan of exasperation, Marnie waited, then
replaced the receiver, praying he'd call again. But the
phone remained utterly and frustratingly silent, and fifteen
minutes later she reluctantly returned to bed. Why had Cal
phoned? What had he wanted to tell her?

Why, after thirteen years, had she opened herself up to
the kind of loneliness and longing that now was keeping
her wide-awake?

Cal, she said silently, I want you, I love you, I need you.
Come home to me, please.

Because, of course, she did love Cal. She knew that now,
without a shadow of a doubt.

Nine days later, when Marnie walked home from school,
she was in a state of high excitement. It was June, the sun
was shining, and Cal was coming home tonight on a ten-
thirty flight. And she and Kit were getting along wonder-
fully well.

They'd spent all of Sunday together last weekend, prac-
ticing on one of the beginner slopes at Eagles's Nest. Then
they'd eaten supper at a Chinese restaurant and talked, really talked, about any number of things. In the middle of
which Kit had said, "Maybe someday you and Dad'll get
married."

Marnie had dropped her fork with a clatter and flushed
scarlet. "Oh, I don't know, that's not...well, what I mean
is—"

"I think it'd be cool if you did that. And I bet Mum
would like the idea, too." Kit's forehead wrinkled in

thought. "She wasn't daring like you, but she always wanted Dad to be happy."

"I know she and your father loved each other," Marnie ventured.

"Yep. He cried when she died, I never knew men cried. It was sort of a shocker. But I think he really likes you." Rather anxiously, Kit added, "I don't want you thinking he's a wimp just because he's scared of heights. One time in the Sudan, he saved the lives of a whole bunch of people by hijacking a truck and getting them out of danger. He's really very brave."

"I know that, Kit."

"We could have ice cream for dessert on the way home," Kit said, swallowing the last of her sweet and sour chicken.

Smiling to herself as she remembered this conversation, Marnie admired the sun's playful dance on the ocean and the tall blue spires of the lupins in the ditch. She turned down her driveway, already going over her wardrobe to see what she'd wear tonight. A dress, perhaps. Something very feminine...

When she walked into the living room, her answering machine was blinking. Quickly, she pressed the button. "Marnie, this is Andrea, Lizzie's mother. I'm afraid I have rather bad news. There's been some kind of uprising around the airport in Kampala, and Cal's flight didn't get away. The embassy doesn't seem to know what's going on yet, but I'll keep you posted as soon as I hear anything. So far I haven't said anything to Kit. My husband and I can't see the point of worrying her. Although if we don't hear by early tomorrow morning, we'll have to tell her. Sorry about this, Marnie. Bye."

Marnie's heart had hardened to a lump of ice in her chest, and she was having difficulty breathing. She pressed the button again, but inexorably the same words came out of her machine. She then flicked through all the news channels, finally picking up on the BBC the mention of a small-scale insurrection, although with no details. It was only a minor incident, she thought wildly. Not worth bothering about.

Except that Cal was there.

Cal, whom she loved.

She paced up and down. She sat out on her deck and stared blankly at the ocean, having left the door open so she'd hear the phone. She ate a sandwich that could have been made of paper and paced some more, with the television on as well as the radio. She went to bed around midnight and lay awake for the better part of the night, praying for the phone to ring.

It did ring at eight the next morning. "Marnie? Andrea. The embassy just called. They seem to think flights will be leaving today and that Cal should be on one of them. Kit wanted to go to school—she says she's better keeping busy—but she sends you her love. She said to be sure I used those exact words. I'll let you know as soon as we hear anything else."

Marnie gave her the number of her school and hung up. Then she sat down hard on the nearest chair, her knees trembling. She had news of Cal, even if it wasn't as precise as she would like. And Kit had sent her love.

She'd been given her daughter back, Marnie thought, and counted herself blessed. Surely she couldn't lose Cal, not now. Not when she and Kit were truly mother and daughter, and happiness was within her grasp. In a single night in her bed, Cal had taught her so much about the ways of love and the intimacy possible between a man and a woman. An intimacy on which they could build a marriage. Couldn't they?

Somehow Marnie got through the day, carrying a lump of anxiety as heavy as a granite boulder everywhere she went, although she was somewhat comforted by Christine's concern. When she pushed open her door, her heart thumping, she saw the green light flashing twice on her machine. Steeling herself, she pushed the Play button.

His voice gravelly with exhaustion, Cal said, "Marnie, I'm in London. The first flight I could get arrives in Halifax at midnight tonight—can you meet me? I'm going to call Kit next and let her know where I am."

The second message was from Andrea, who jubilantly left the same information.

Then, as though she'd conjured it up, the phone shrilled. This time it was Kit. "I just got home from school and Dad's safe. He's in London and he'll get into Halifax at midnight. Marnie, will you meet the plane?"

It must be true, Marnie thought. He must be safe. Three people were telling her he was. "Yes…yes, I'll meet him."

Obviously striving to sound matter-of-fact, Kit said, "I expect he'll be really tired. It's okay with me if he wants to stay at your place instead of driving all the way home. I'll stay at Lizzie's and see him tomorrow. Will you tell him that?"

Not sure if she wanted to laugh or cry, Marnie said, "I'll see what he wants to do. I'm just so glad he's safe."

"Me, too. Can we have another climbing lesson on Sunday?"

"I'd like that…and Kit, thanks for sending your love. I love you, too."

It was the first time she'd said this. Kit answered with unaccustomed shyness, "That's good. See you soon."

The next seven hours felt like seven days. Marnie cleaned her house from one end to the other, ate supper, showered and tried on five different outfits before settling

on a slim silk skirt with a purple overblouse that fell grace-
fully to her hips. It made her look sophisticated and more
sure of herself than she felt; and it went with her newly
painted purple toenails.

What if Cal had decided while he was away that he
wasn't willing to risk loving her? What if that had been the
gist of that frustrating phone call? How could she bear it?

Trying to concentrate on details, Marnie put on makeup,
slingback pumps and her gold jewelry, and knew she was
as ready as she'd ever be. She drove straight to the airport,
her hands welded to the steering wheel, arriving an hour
early because she was so afraid she'd be late. In the washroom mirror, she saw a woman who looked like a stranger,
her eyes brilliant with nervousness, her body a series of
lissome curves in an outfit that made her look both mysterious and glamorous.

She should've worn her jeans, she thought in a panic.
Cal was used to her in jeans and shorts, not in slinky silk.

She was behaving more like Kit than a woman of thirty
who supposedly knew her own mind. One thing she did
know: she couldn't skulk in the washroom for an hour.

As the digital clock clicked off the minutes with agoniz-
ing slowness, Marnie tried very hard to concentrate on a
magazine someone had left on the chair. Then, finally, the
screen indicated Cal's flight had arrived. Fifteen minutes
later, the door from Customs swung open and the first passengers trickled through. Marnie stationed herself as close
as she could get without impeding the travelers' progress,
her hands as cold as ice.

Cal was the fifth one through the door. He was limping.
He looked awful.

He saw her immediately, and something that had been
tightly guarded in his face relaxed. He closed the distance
between them, put his suitcase down and took her in his

arms, burying his fingers in her hair before kissing her with
an explicitness not entirely suitable for an airport terminal.

Not that Marnie was complaining. His body was hard
and warm against hers, she would have known the smell
of his skin anywhere in the world, and it was sheer heaven
to be held by him again.

Dropping tiny kisses around her mouth, Cal said,
"Marnie, I love you. Will you marry me?"

She gaped up at him, wondering if she'd heard him right.
"Whatever happened to your face?"

"I got in a fight. Several, actually. Answer the question."

"You're giving me orders again."

His grin made him look thoroughly raffish. "I can't get
down on my knees. I got bashed on the thigh with a chunk
of wood. But it's obvious I need to live with a strong-
minded woman who won't let me order her around. Marry
me, Marnie."

"Is that another order?" She looped her arms around his
neck, carefully avoiding his scraped cheek and luridly
bruised cheekbone. "It could be a life's work."

"Oh, I'd want it to be."

"You figure I can do it?"

"I'm putty in your hands," he said solemnly.

She laughed outright. "Now that I doubt, Cal
Huntingdon. But it's my turn to give the orders. Tell me
again that you love me."

He cupped her face in his palms, kissing her once more,
totally ignoring the influx of passengers that swirled around
them. "I love you so much I can hardly breathe," he said.
"I figured that out between London and Uganda on the
way out there, called you as soon as we landed and wasn't
even sure I'd gotten through to you. Serves me right, no
doubt."

She said, nuzzling her cheek into his shoulder, "That phone call kept me awake all night. Kiss me again and you're forgiven."

With an ardor that was more than satisfactory, he complied. "We walked smack into some kind of minicoup last night on the way to the airport. There were a couple of hours when I wasn't sure I was going to make it out of there in one piece—that I'd be able to tell you face-to-face that I love you with all my heart and want to spend the rest of my life with you. That I've finally worked out that love's far more powerful than loss. I'd left it too late. Those have to be the two worst words in the whole language. Too late."

"It's not too late, Cal," Marnie said shakily. "Because I love you, too. More than I can say."

His face stilled. "You do?"

She said the words out loud that she'd repeated like a mantra ten days ago. "I love you, I want you, I need you."

"Enough to marry me?"

"Oh, yes," she said, and kissed him as though he'd been away for ten months rather than ten days. Then she said, "Let's get out of here and go home. We can talk on the way."

"Home's wherever you are," he said.

Arms around each other, they walked out to her car. As Cal climbed in, taking his time, Marnie said, "You'd better tell me what happened. Because you're hurting, I can see."

"The coup was a very amateurish attempt, although I never did find out the details. On the road into the city, a group of kids were being mistreated by a gang of looters, so the five of us intervened. I used every dirty trick I know, and I know a few. The kids got away and eventually we made it to the airport, where we hung out until the planes started flying again this morning."

"And that," Marnie said, "is a very condensed version."

"It's all you're getting. But there's nothing like seeing someone do his best to bash your brains in to make you realize where your priorities lie. Mine are here with you—that's what I learned and that's where I want to be. Now and forever." He eased back in the seat as she drove toward the exit kiosk. "I'm almost sure Kit'll be okay with our getting married...what do you think?"

"Kit suggested to me after we climbed the Eagles's Nest last Sunday that you and I might like to get married. She also said you ought to stay at my house tonight. Because you'd be tired."

Cal gave a choked laugh. "When she comes around, she does a good job of it. Marnie, I hate to sound unromantic, but I can count on both hands the hours of sleep I've had the past week—wake me when we get to your place, will you?" And he closed his eyes.

They were dark shadowed, and from the extreme care with which he'd climbed into the car, Marnie was quite sure there was a lot Cal wasn't saying. Filled with deep gratitude that he was alive, and with wonderment and joy that he loved her as much as she loved him, she drove back to her little house by the sea. Pulling up by the door, she said softly, "Cal, we're home."

He woke instantly. "Lead me to the shower," he said, yawning.

She let him into the house, feeling oddly shy for a woman who'd been very nicely proposed to. She busied herself getting out clean towels and noticed he didn't ask her to shower with him. In her bedroom, she changed into her prettiest nightgown, which had a scalloped neckline that exposed her cleavage and long slits up either side that exposed her thighs, and sat down on her bed to brush her hair.

She heard the bathroom door open, then Cal walked into the bedroom, a towel swathed around his hips. "It looks worse than it is," he said uncomfortably. "The doc in London said nothing was broken."

She looked at him in silence, from the livid bruises on his thigh and ribs to the jagged cut on his arm, whose edges had been neatly stitched together. She said quietly, "Loving you makes me terribly vulnerable."

He sat down beside her, resting his hands on her bare shoulders. "The same's true for me. Perhaps it's called living dangerously."

She burst out, "I promise I won't try to climb Everest if you promise you won't go to the world's ten most dangerous places."

"Done," Cal agreed.

"I do love you," Marnie said, stroking a lock of hair back from his grazed forehead.

Cal said huskily, "It's past time I show you how much I love you."

She said dubiously, "You don't look in great shape—we could always go to sleep." With an impish smile, she added, "After all, we've got the rest of our lives. Oh, Cal, isn't that wonderful, amazing and incredible? The rest of our lives! So I really don't mind if we go to sleep now."

"We'll go to sleep later," Cal replied firmly, and through the pale satin of her nightgown took her breasts in his hands, bending to kiss her on the lips.

"Not that you're giving orders," Marnie said, and kissed him back.

As Cal had once said to her, one thing led to another; it was quite a while before they fell asleep.

The next morning, Kit was delighted to hear that they were getting married.

As was Christine.

You're not going to believe this offer!

In October and November 2000, buy any two Harlequin or Silhouette books and save $10.00 off future purchases, or buy any three and save $20.00 off future purchases!

Just fill out this form and attach 2 proofs of purchase (cash register receipts) from October and November 2000 books and Harlequin will send you a coupon booklet worth a total savings of $10.00 off future purchases of Harlequin and Silhouette books in 2001. Send us 3 proofs of purchase and we will send you a coupon booklet worth a total savings of $20.00 off future purchases.

Saving money has never been this easy.

I accept your offer! Please send me a coupon booklet:

Name: _____

Address: _____ City: _____

State/Prov.: _____ Zip/Postal Code: _____

Optional Survey!

In a typical month, how many Harlequin or Silhouette books would you buy <u>new</u> at retail stores?

☐ Less than 1 ☐ 1 ☐ 2 ☐ 3 to 4 ☐ 5+

Which of the following statements best describes how you <u>buy</u> Harlequin or Silhouette books? Choose one answer only that <u>best</u> describes you.

☐ I am a regular buyer and reader
☐ I am a regular reader but buy only occasionally
☐ I only buy and read for specific times of the year, e.g. vacations
☐ I subscribe through Reader Service but also buy at retail stores
☐ I mainly borrow and buy only occasionally
☐ I am an occasional buyer and reader

Which of the following statements best describes how you <u>choose</u> the Harlequin and Silhouette series books you buy <u>new</u> at retail stores? By "series," we mean books within a particular line, such as *Harlequin PRESENTS* or *Silhouette SPECIAL EDITION*. Choose one answer only that <u>best</u> describes you.

☐ I only buy books from my favorite series
☐ I generally buy books from my favorite series but also buy books from other series on occasion
☐ I buy some books from my favorite series but also buy from many other series regularly
☐ I buy all types of books depending on my mood and what I find interesting and have no favorite series

---

Please send this form, along with your cash register receipts as proofs of purchase, to:
In the U.S.: Harlequin Books, P.O. Box 9057, Buffalo, NY 14269
In Canada: Harlequin Books, P.O. Box 622, Fort Erie, Ontario L2A 5X3
(Allow 4-6 weeks for delivery) Offer expires December 31, 2000.

PHQ4002

If you enjoyed what you just read,
then we've got an offer you can't resist!

Take 2 bestselling
love stories FREE!
Plus get a FREE surprise gift!